ALIEN CODEX

LIVE ALIEN CONTACT
BOOK 2

LEAH R CUTTER

KNOTTED ROAD PRESS

Reviews
It's true. Reviews help me sell more books. If you've enjoyed this story, please consider leaving a review of it on your favorite site.

Come someplace new...
Do you enjoy exploring strange new worlds, new cultures, new people?

Journey into the various lands envisioned by Leah R Cutter.

Sign up for my newsletter and I'll start you on your travels with a free copy of my book, *The Island Sampler*.

http://www.LeahCutter.com/newsletter/

Buy More!
Did you know that you can buy directly from the Knotted Road Press website?

https://www.knottedroadpress.com/shop/

Circle of Water

Circle of Earth

Seattle Trolls

The Changeling Troll

The Princess Troll

The Fairy-Bridge Troll

The Troll-Demon War

The Troll-Human War

The Troll-Troll War

The Shadow Wars Trilogy

The Raven and the Dancing Tiger

The Guardian Hound

War Among the Crocodiles

The Clockwork Fairy Kingdom

The Clockwork Fairy Kingdom

The Maker, the Teacher, and the Monster

The Dwarven Wars

The Cassie Stories

Poisoned Pearls

Tainted Waters

Spoiled Harvest

Bloodied Ice

The Chronicles of Franklin

Franklin Versus The Popcorn Thief

Franklin Versus The Soul Thief

Franklin Versus The Child Thief

Epic Fantasy Series

The Fallen Elves

Ruins of the Gods

Stairs of the Gods

Cities of the Gods

Graves of the Gods

Houses of the Dead

Houses Divided

Houses Fallen

Houses Reborn

Forgotten Gods

A Wind Blown Torment

A Stone Strewn Clash

A Sea Washed Victory

The Tanesh Empire Trilogy

The Glass Magician

The Desert Heart

The Ghost Dog

Mysteries

The Purloined Letter Opener

The Tell-Tale Heart Pin

Dancer in Darkness

Trophy Hunters

The Alvin Goodfellow Case Files

The Rabbit Mysteries

The Shredded Veil Mysteries

Mystery, Crime, and Mayhem

ONE

Rosey wasn't exactly sure what to expect when they arrived at the ass-end of nowhere in terms of known space. Tyrone, the planet they were approaching, was at the far reaches of Allied Worlds space.

Though the Allied Worlds barely counted as a government —more like a mob of barely restrained warlords. On the other hand, they were better than the assholes that ran the Kollective, that group of old stodgies in charge of the government closest to Earth.

A part of her had anticipated that someone would have hailed her starship *The Roadrunner* and insisted that she pay fees to the local protection racket to ensure safe passage for her ship. Or maybe some level of corrupt bureaucracy, demanding bribes.

Technically, that had been what happened.

Some punk named Ajax had hailed her when she'd first entered the system. Turned out, he'd followed her previous career as a speedship racer, and had recognized her and her ship when they'd entered the system.

Now, he wanted to race her in that jacked-up rusting garbage heap over there, *Hermes 3.0.* It was either win the race or pay Ajax off.

She couldn't back down, either. Not if they wanted to actually make it to the planet. *The Roadrunner* had a couple of small guns for deflecting asteroids or space debris. Nothing like the armaments the other ship had.

Rosey, Moe, and Atilio had made the trip from the planet Psykee together, chasing after Oswald, the techno-wizard who'd stolen Rosie's alien computer components. It had only taken them ten hours of flying through hyperspace to get there.

Quite frankly, Rosey was still shaking off the aftereffects of spending so much time in another dimension. Going through hyperspace felt like stepping into reality sideways, with all the colors, temperatures, and lights askew enough to make a person start questioning their sanity.

"Dennis, do you think we can beat this punk?" Rosie asked her ship's AI.

She was seated in the cockpit located at the front of her ship. This was one of the areas of the ship that she hadn't allowed Dennis to endlessly redecorate. (Who knew that a ship's AI would develop such a distinct passion?)

As a result, the pilot's couch was a basic, off-white material that Dennis frequently complained about, the controls were factory-standard colors, and the walls were gray steel. (All right, so Rosey may have buffed them up so they shone. She didn't mind the hard lines but they had been a little plain.) She had allowed Dennis to reconfigure all the air vents. He claimed that it just improved the *feng shui* of the entire ship. She appreciated the better air flow. The fans were all turned up high to help her recover from hyperspace, the feel of a breeze helping to settle her back in her body, as it were.

"I'm certain you've tuned my engines tight enough this last passage," Dennis said sourly.

"What? I always want you to have that fighting edge," Rosey replied.

The pair of them had an agreement: Dennis had free reign to design (and redesign) most of the interior of *The Roadrunner,* while she got to tweak his engines constantly. Plus, refit the ship with the best hyperspace shielding credits could buy. They could stay in hyperspace for ten hours safely. Maybe eleven, if she was pushing it. Not twelve, or the ship would be shredded and no one left alive.

Both Rosey and Dennis had budgets for their projects. Moderate work could be done without buy-in from the other. Extensive work required agreement beforehand. (Though Rosey had the feeling that Dennis didn't actually understand the word *moderate.*)

While flying to Tyrone, Rosey and Atilio had spent some time working on Dennis's engines. It was nice to have a competent mechanic at hand. He was about the same height as her, five foot seven, also in his mid-fifties. While Rosey's curls had turned white, Atilio's were just starting to gray. Plus, Rosey had more of an athletic build from years doing manual labor and martial arts, and Atilio at least appeared to be carrying a bit of extra weight around. Not much, as he was former military, and could still drop down and give you forty without breaking a sweat.

However, he did follow the wrong religion. Really, who used the Dillinger yellow toolset anymore? Anyone who knew anything used the red tools from Badger instead.

"Scans show a secondary engine in our opponent's spaceship," Dennis said after a few moments. "So he might have a surprise burst of speed mid-course."

Hmm. While such engines weren't allowed in speedships, she'd seen such non-legal engines in local competitions, where contestants didn't have to follow the official racing rules.

It wasn't that much of an advantage, though, at least as far as Rosey was concerned. Courses were computer generated and required finesse as well as the ability to change direction easily, not just speed.

Rosey considered the ship over there again, not paying attention to her readouts as much as what her eyes showed her.

Dennis had a skinny front end and a big ass due to the reconfigured cargo bays. Rosey no longer raced, but instead, built speedships for clients. She could deliver up to four at a time in *The Roadrunner*.

The ship facing her—*Hermes 3.0*—had two curving prongs sticking out at the front—maybe a primary and a secondary helm. The back of the ship was big and boxy, probably living quarters and engines. Plus the weapon turrets stuck out in all directions, looking something like a crab who'd mated with a porcupine.

Because of its vaguely circular shape, *Hermes 3.0* might be able to take the side-to-side turns in a slalom course better than *The Roadrunner*. During any straight sections, *The Roadrunner* would be faster, even if the other ship had a secondary engine system. The question would be at the midpoint, when the ships had to turn all the way around. How fast could *Hermes 3.0* make that turn?

What couldn't be seen on the scans, but only showed up to the eye, was how poorly maintained *Hermes 3.0* appeared to be. Rosey was serious in that it looked like a rust bucket. The hull had been patched at various times using different colored materials. When she zoomed in, she could see the mis-placed bolts.

She was personally offended. If you're going to redneck something together, at least do it with style.

The exterior of *The Roadrunner* was sleek and fit, uniform and modern. She used the same porcelain alloy on the exterior of her ship that she used on speedships.

And yes, it might have had a hint of red color, as well as something of a shimmer to it.

Red ones do go faster, you know.

"All right, *Hermes 3.0*, you got yourself a race," Rosie said eventually.

"Really?" Ajax squealed. "I get to race you?" He paused, cleared his throat, then continued in a deeper, calmer tone. "I mean, of course. Follow me to the area designated for racing, where you're going to lose."

Rosey snorted. She knew exactly how to deal with that fanboy over there. Even if he lost, the fact that he'd gotten a chance to race *her* would still give him immense bragging rights.

And he would lose.

Rosey had more than one trick up her sleeve.

Atilio and Moe—Rosey's passengers—were suited up in stretchsuits, in case of an accident. They were also strapped into crash couches in the back. While Rosey had told them this was in case something went wrong, really, she just didn't want to be disturbed while in the middle of a run. She'd routed the front screen vid back to them, so they could watch her race in real time.

Once they were taken care of, she followed *Hermes 3.0* to an area on the far side of the planet Tyrone.

A regular competition-style space awaited her. The course itself would be generated by a competition speedracer computer. As far as both Rosey and Dennis could tell, that equipment hadn't been modified or gamed.

Someone had paid a lot of credits to set this up, as well as paying what were surely annual licensing and inspection fees.

Why set up such a system out here, so far off the circuit? No official races would be held this far off the beaten track.

Maybe this was where locals trained in order to join the race circuit.

It wasn't until Rosey saw all the smaller ships, flitters and spaceships, those that either came from the planet below or from somewhere in the system, that she realized what she was dealing with.

Tyrone had a huge racing fanbase. No wonder Ajax had recognized her right away, when she'd entered the system.

The Roadrunner was being scanned by every ship that had the capacity, to ascertain that it was her, really truly *her*, at the helm.

Hopefully, she'd be able to use her reputation to her advantage.

The area they'd race in wasn't that big—it was about the same size as the space that Rosey used to test the speedships she built. The course itself would be randomly generated by the race computer and sent to the competitors seconds before they began.

Rosey knew what to look for when the map was streamed to *The Roadrunner*. While some racers flipped to the end of the course to see the final section, Rosey always paid attention to the start.

If she could get the jump on her competitors, put a little

fear into their hearts, that would stand her better than some elaborate strategy that might or might not unfold at the end.

This course started off with a slalom that went up and down, not side to side. This section, it was a tossup as to which ship would make it through more cleanly.

Good.

Rosey had made special adjustments to *The Roadrunner* so that the ship could quickly jump into a race, getting up to speed faster than the original specs would indicate. She grasped the pilot's yoke lightly, fingers poised over the buttons on the edges that manipulated gyros and speed. Her stretchsuit felt like a second skin, keeping her body temperature perfectly regulated (none of those nasty adrenaline sweat stains for her, thank you very much).

When the lights on her screen went green, Rosey rammed the yoke forward. *The Roadrunner* leaped ahead, racing toward the first buoy.

Hermes 3.0 made a good effort, catching up to her after they'd crested the first buoy and were headed down toward the second.

However, it was obvious from the start that Ajax over there wasn't a top-notch racer. He didn't skim the buoy like Rosey did. There was a lot of wasted space between his ship and the marker.

And in a race like this, space equaled time.

Next, came a squiggly set of curves. It took precise timing to make it through the markers set up on either side, to not go too fast and lose control, but also to not go too slow and lose ground. Unfortunately, as Rosey had anticipated, *Hermes 3.0* handled the side-to-side movement well. The lead she'd built up at the start was quickly lost.

The two ships exited the curves nose and nose, bombing down the straightaway, toward the turning point.

Ajax didn't turn on his secondary engines at that time. Good. That showed some smarts, because a racer had to decelerate in order to make that midway turn.

Rosey dipped down below the marker, then braked and pulled back hard on the yoke, forcing the nose of *The Roadrunner* up and around, flying back over the marker upside-down before straightening herself out.

Ajax copied the move exactly.

Hrumph.

Was she getting predictable? That would never do.

A second slalom course faced the contestants as they finished the midturn point. This time, the ships needed to go from side-to-side.

For the first time, *Hermes 3.0* pulled out ahead of *The Roadrunner*.

Rosey growled and gritted her teeth.

She was not about to let some punk from the ass-end of nowhere beat her.

If he did, she might as well truly retire.

Then what was she going to do? Learn how to knit?

They now were racing back toward the planet Abruptly, Rosey's view of it was replaced with a series of dots that expanded rapidly.

Crap.

The computer had generated one of Rosey's least favorite racing segments for the next part: the obstacle course.

This one was an asteroid field. Other options she'd seen included racing over the surface of a sun and having to avoid eruptions, flying in between battling ships and darting around shots as well as debris, and even a mine field where the racer was following some idiot who kept accidently setting off the stupid mines.

This wasn't a real asteroid field. Most of those were completely harmless, with the larger asteroids miles apart, steady in their orbit, and easy to avoid.

No, this was a made-up one, meant to be exciting, at least for the fans viewing the race.

Rosey had seen more than one moron wreck their speed-ship by trying to skim the big rocks which were not smooth, or getting themselves twisted around with their maneuvers.

She took a deep breath, settling herself. Fans kicked on, blowing air directly into her face. A calm descended over her. For the first time, she felt the *flow* of the race taking over. She became one with the ship, dancing between the spinning rocks, effortlessly shifting up, sideways, and down.

Rosey knew better than to take this sort of course at full speed. She'd end up in a simulated crash and lose the race.

Hermes 3.0 had entered the obstacle course before she did, but lost ground quickly. Poor punk hadn't flown as many of these as Rosey had.

Rosey exited the obstacle course three point two seconds ahead of her competition.

However, the last segment turned out to be a second straightaway.

It was the best possible setup for a ship like *Hermes 3.0*, particularly if they had a secondary engine set that they could bring online.

"We gotta hustle," Rosey snapped at Dennis as she entered the last course segment. She tapped the button for more speed, pressing the yoke forward.

The ship didn't respond how it should have. Everything felt sluggish.

"What's the magic word?" Dennis taunted.

Hermes 3.0 kicked on their secondary engines. Suddenly, the two ships were nose and nose.

"Are you kidding me?" Rosey yelled. She shook the yoke in frustration. Pressed on it. Actually made a bit of a turn, just to try to throw off her competition, get him to have to slow down and curve away from her a bit.

He wasn't having any of it. He continued to bomb ahead.

Young punk probably thought he was immortal or something equally asinine.

"I'm waiting," Dennis sang out.

Rosey gave an expressive sigh. "Fine. Please. Pile on the power. Now. Or we're going to lose."

"Well, since you asked so nicely," Dennis said.

Suddenly, *The Roadrunner* leaped ahead. Rosey wasn't sure where all the power was coming from. She hadn't made that many adjustments to the engines, had she?

In the end, it was still a close race. *The Roadrunner* did win, clearing the finish line two full seconds ahead of *Hermes 3.0.*

"Do you want to hear your adoring crowds?" Dennis asked.

"Sure," Rosey said dryly. She didn't need that commentary, not as much as she once did. Dennis, she was certain, was dying to hear it.

As Rosey had suspected, there was indeed a *huge* racing fanbase out there. They were thrilled with the race and already starting to dissect every move that each racer had made. They accused her of playing a game with *Hermes 3.0,* letting him catch up and thinking he could win, before piling on the speed.

No matter. Always agree with a commenter when they called you sneaky.

Hermes 3.0 hailed her after some of the roar had died down.

"Wow. Thank you for the race," Ajax said sincerely.

"You're welcome," Rosey said. She needed to keep her reflexes tuned, particularly given the nature of her mission.

"So what brings you out to Tyrone?" Ajax asked after a few moments. "Is there anything I can help you with?"

Rosey grinned. "Yes, as a matter of fact, there is."

Having local intelligence on Oswald was going to be invaluable.

If she played this right, she might have a team of racers willing to go to battle for her as well.

TWO

Princess Jun Ogawa sat quietly on her side of the dining table, listening to Jamaal Akintola spin tales, entertaining the military ship's captain, the second-in-command, and the other officers gathered there. He seemed to know exactly how to play to his audience, the sorts of adventures they'd like to hear.

He was quite good at deflecting attention away from what he didn't want to talk about, namely, how *he* had been the one who'd found her, as well as what he and Rosey had been doing.

Jun still had questions, though.

She had finally traded in her archaeological digger's comfortable shirt, baggy pants with lots of pockets, and hooded cloak, for something more befitting a princess. The underlayer was a modified stretchsuit that covered her completely. The material was similar to sharkskin armor and would deflect most weapons. The main body of the suit was done in the dark green of the Empire, with gold material that went from elbows to wrists, as well as from knees to ankles. Over that, she wore a billowing white robe with inch-wide black accents around every seam. She'd put on her "princess paint" as she called it, wearing full makeup: the base smoothed out her tan skin until it was without pores or blemishes; bright red dabs of color on her upper and lower lips, right in the center, giving her the iconic (and supposedly beautiful) "fish lips"; and black lines around her brown eyes, in a cat's eye style.

Honestly, she felt ridiculous, like a brightly colored doll, particularly compared to the dull greens and browns the military people wore.

But that was also the point. She was Important People, and in some ways, outranked everyone on the ship. And it was supposed to show.

She'd been handed a new AI necklace when she'd boarded the military vessel. However, it only contained a small sliver of the original Sano personality, and so she wasn't interacting with it much. The necklace that contained all of Sano was still on Moe's ship *Aisha*.

That version of Sano had all of Jun's notes about the Atoylee, one of only two extinct alien races that Humanity had run across in all their years of space travel.

Jun had left Sano behind on the ship when the warlord Constantine's thugs had suddenly appeared. She hadn't had much time to secure the necklace. She'd run as soon as she'd seen the men, murmuring command words to Sano, shutting her down completely.

Anyone trying to break into the AI's system would receive the warning that if they continued, all the systems on the device would be permanently trashed. All that would remain for the would-be hacker was an inoperable, gaudy-looking bauble.

Jun had had a particular place in mind as she'd raced away from Constantine's goons. She'd tossed the necklace into

Atilio's room, throwing it under his bed as she'd passed the door, still running.

The goons had her trapped soon after that, coming at her from both ends of the hallway.

After Jun had hidden Sano, she'd resentfully surrendered, making them believe that she'd had someplace else she'd wanted to go, to hide in.

While the goons chasing her hadn't initially believed her when she'd told them she was Princess Jun Ogawa, they'd at least been smart enough to check on her story before roughing her up.

Or worse.

Jun wouldn't allow her feelings about the warlord Constantine free rein. Or she might scare the nice military men sitting there.

A princess wasn't supposed to be that angry. No, she was always supposed to exude control, serenity, and personal power.

However, Constantine hadn't just stolen all the alien Atoylee artifacts that her people had uncovered that year on the planet Niani. He'd also taken all their notes as well. Some of those hadn't been scanned, and were the only copies.

She was certain that she was on the verge of a serious break-through when it came to figuring out what had happened to the Atoylee, who they'd been fighting, and why their planet had been destroyed.

It was all tied up on the moon Lawaka, and the secret base that the Atoylee had had there. No one had ever taken a really serious look at the closer of the two moons around Niani before, as researchers had only ever speculated that the Atoylee had built on the moon. Plus, it was much easier to mount an archaeological dig on an actual planet with gravity and breathable air than on a waterless hunk of rock with no atmosphere.

Still. Jun knew she had to go back, had to figure out that puzzle.

After she paid her respects on Ishiman, of course.

Beyond being told that her brother Minato was sick, there hadn't been much news of her family.

Jamaal had started in on yet another tall tale. His dark skin shone under the bright lights, and his kinky black hair was sheared close to his scalp. He was currently wearing a bright orange robe with gold braid around the standing collar as well as the cuffs and the bottom hem. The robe went down to his wrists and swirled around his feet when he walked.

Sano had told Jun that it was made of a high-quality silk-blend that regulated temperature, ensuring that the wearer was never too hot or too cold. That made it much more expensive than it looked.

While Jamaal's eyes held merriment, as well as intelligence, Jun had also noticed a certain wariness to them. Anytime they walked into a new room on the military escort taking them to the Emperor's court, he automatically categorized all the entrances, exits, sightlines, and potential weapons.

He reminded her of Itsuki, the Emperor's spy master. Itsuki's official position in court was that of the high priest of the God of Fire, one of the myriad spirits that the court was required to ritually sacrifice to. Few knew his true work. Most of the time, Itsuki was in the background, silent and ever watching.

The two men weren't anything alike. Jamaal was so loud, always drawing attention to himself. Itsuki was the opposite— so quiet you'd forget that he was in the room.

However, the watching quality that they both had was eerily similar.

In addition, Jamaal had yet to actually answer Jun about how he'd happened to find her. This "friend of a friend" who'd called in a favor while he'd been in the neighborhood wasn't the full truth.

So Jun pretended to be entertained along with the others. She could get her answers later, such as who Jamaal actually was, and how he'd gotten access to alien artifacts from an obscure alien race that no one else had encountered.

Jun had agreed to not say anything more about those. In return for her silence, Jamaal had promised to take her back to the others when he left, not to just abandon her on Ishiman, the planet of the Emperor's Court.

She *had* to get back to the others.

Particularly if Jamaal's aliens turned out to be some figment of his imagination. Or if Rosey couldn't get back the alien artifacts that some techno-genius had stolen from her.

So Jun sat. Listened. Schemed.

And didn't allow herself to think about Moe, his poet's eyes, his sad smile, or how he'd given up everything just to save her.

THREE

Atilio sat on the crash couch aboard *The Roadrunner*, strapped in, as he watched Rosey finish the race with *Hermes 3.0*. While Atilio didn't know that much about racing—it had never been a sport that he'd followed—he did know something about flying.

And crazy-assed pilots.

The obstacle course had been the most surprising portion of the course, as well as the most revealing. He hadn't known about that, hadn't realized those could be a segment of a race. Made sense, though. There were probably other versions of an obstacle course that racers trained on.

When Atilio had served in the Emperor's military, the pilots he'd known had their own insane training regimes. He'd been told about a type of Hogan's Alley, basically, a gauntlet that a battle cruiser had to fly through while being attacked on either side by various other ships. He didn't understand it, never wanted to have to go through that kind of thing more than once, but he respected their determination.

His estimation of Rosey had risen as well, watching her

handle that asteroid belt. Sure, it was a made up thing. She'd still slide the ship around every asteroid, anticipating the next obstacle in her course, then dancing with it as well.

Atilio didn't know of many pilots who could have done it as gracefully. Even the really crazy ones.

Atilio had been a sergeant, in command of a troop of engineers, as well as a few regular military types, there to protect the rude bastards.

He'd learned early on that the best way to motivate the people reporting to him was to challenge them, tell them something couldn't be done.

They'd move heaven and earth to prove him wrong.

He suspected that Rosey was only slightly more sane. If something really was impossible, she'd tell him. Otherwise, she'd probably just be excited by the challenge.

Atilio had loved the army. Loved not having to think or plan ahead. Long-range planning was for fancy commissioned officers. All he had to do was to execute orders.

He was damned good at that.

The Empire wasn't at war with anyone—the Allied Worlds were too poor, the Kollective too inward facing, and Emperor Ogawa knew better. Wars were expensive, hard to win, and generally, not worth it.

There were still areas of unrest though, where one country decided to squabble with the next, or one planet reached a little too far in terms of dominating its neighbors.

Atilio and his people would ensure that everyone saw sense in the end. Plus there had been more than once when they'd been deployed to help deal with a local disaster: tornadoes, hurricanes, earthquakes, what have you.

However, then he'd run into some officers who'd stopped

trying to do the right thing. Who were no longer looking at the greater good, but only for personal gain.

Maybe Atilio had been naïve. That was certainly the opinion of the other sergeants.

He'd still made it his mission to get those damned officers removed, their "good" names blackened and ruined, all the filth of their deeds sticking to them.

Unfortunately, though the upper-ups understood that Atilio had done the right thing and deserved a god-damned medal, they'd still forced him to take an honorable discharge.

And then dumped him where he was, in the middle of Allied Worlds' territory, without a clue or a plan.

Sure, if he'd scrimped and saved he could have lived out the rest of his life on that planet, given his pension.

That wasn't his idea of a good life.

Then fate had dropped Moe in his lap, just before the cheap vodka really took hold and he'd lost all the muscles and conditioning he'd spent hours sweating over.

Moe wasn't a great leader. However, he gave Atilio a compass, places to go, a job he could do. A ship he could call home.

Atilio had had doubts about Rosey being able to help them get *Aisha* back. Now, having watched her race this punk, as well as listening to the locals and their breathless commentary about the race, he knew that she was more than capable of beating Constantine's goons if they started chasing them, after they stole *Aisha* from whatever shipyard she sat in.

All they had to do was to grab the ship.

If Constantine hadn't turned *Aisha* into slag. Atilio wouldn't put it past the bastard.

"Whatcha think, boss?" Atilio asked Moe who was sitting beside him. They were both wearing the red stretchsuits that

Rosey had provided. High quality ones, that she had on hand for customers who wanted to do a run with a speedship and hadn't thought to bring their own. Her initials, RDV, were embroidered on the left side of the chest.

Atilio wasn't resentful of Rosey's wealth. He'd helped her work on the engines, knew that she wasn't some pampered princess who'd had everything handed to her. She was smart, funny, good looking, in shape, and so far out of his league it wasn't funny.

Him pursuing her was about as hopeless as Moe and his princess.

"Do you think we could ever get *Aisha* into this good of flying condition?" Moe mused.

"Not without a complete overhaul," Atilio said honestly. "Replace the engines. Reskin the exterior. Probably have to gut the existing flight control system—just an upgrade wouldn't do."

"That's what I thought," Moe said with a sigh. "Maybe someday."

"Maybe someday," Atilio easily agreed. He knew it would never happen. When Moe had his next streak of luck—and he would—the money would go to his family. Or to some poor schmo with a good sob story. If Atilio was lucky, Moe would listen to him and would pay off another chunk of the ship's loan.

Moe could talk to everyone. Could talk the shirt off someone's back.

Didn't. As he'd said more than once, he never wanted to become *that guy.*

Atilio hoped that the universe would continue giving them breaks, that Moe's luck would come back often enough that his captain didn't have to become someone he didn't want to be.

"Should we go congratulate Rosey on her win?" Moe said, already unstrapping himself.

"Naw, give her a few minutes to come down from the rush of the race," Atilio said.

Chances were, Rosey would need more time than that to come back from wherever it was that she'd gone when she'd danced with the ship.

So Moe and Atilio, still in their borrowed stretchsuits, made their way to the kitchen nook, Moe helping himself to some chai tea that he declared was of excellent quality.

"Hey, Dennis," Atilio called as he sat down with his water (that was filtered and pure, unlike the stuff on *Aisha* that always maintained a touch of staleness, no matter how often he cleaned the filters), "what did you think of the race?"

"She hasn't lost it," Dennis said solemnly. "She's still the best. Able to beat me most of the time."

"That's impressive," Atilio told the AI. He wasn't really surprised, though. While AIs could be massively intelligent, and compute all the angles, they didn't have that *instinct* that a Human fighter or pilot had.

"She's still concerned about a possible shimmy in the rear end. Happened at the start of the curves," Dennis said.

"Show me," Atilio said.

Dennis blanked out one of the walls in the nook and displayed a screen instead of the white-painted brick. "Right here," he said, showing a replay of the race from an exterior camera—probably footage from one of the various news stations that had come out to watch.

Dennis slowed down the speed until *The Roadrunner* was crawling along.

"There," Atilio said. "I see it."

"Ah, good," Dennis said. "I suppose Rosey will enlist your help tightening those gyros."

"You don't sound pleased with that," Atilio said. The last thing he wanted to do was to get between a pilot and her ship. That was stupid territory to stray into.

"No, I appreciate her fine-tuning the engines. She just gets them cranked down a little too tight, you know?" Dennis said.

Atilio wasn't really sure what Dennis was implying, so he merely nodded. "I'll see if I can get her to loosen up some."

"Really? Do you think you could talk her into getting me an expanded design budget?" Dennis asked. "I mean, I was acting as a diplomatic carrier when we had the princess on board. That should be reflected in the hallways, don't you believe? I'm thinking lush. Nothing over the top. Maybe just a few lines of gold along the new crown molding."

"Sure, that won't be over the top at all," Rosey said as she entered the area, rolling her eyes. "Ship hallways do not need crown molding."

Moe leaned over to Atilio as Rosey and Dennis continued arguing. "What is crown molding?"

"I'm so glad you asked!" Dennis said. He brought up a picture of the front entranceway of the ship, then flew in pieces of decorative trim along the top of the wall, butted against the ceiling.

"I don't know," Atilio said. "Looks mighty fancy."

Both Rosey and Dennis said, "Exactly!" Though Rosey sounded as if she thought the fancy was too much, while Dennis sounded as if it would be utterly appropriate.

Rosey grabbed her own container of water and sat down at the small eating table with the pair of them. She was glowing from her race, a sparkle in her eyes that made Atilio's heart warm.

"So we're going to be meeting with Ajax in an hour or so," Rosey said. "Moe, I want you to come with me and negotiate."

"All right," Moe said slowly, nodding. "Why?"

"Gotta earn your keep. And I haven't forgotten about going back and helping you break *Aisha* out of jail."

"You're the face guy, boss," Atilio added, unrepentant. "You'll get us a good deal."

Rosey nodded in approval. "Exactly. And Atilio—"

"Dennis already pointed out the one shimmy in the turn," Atilio said. "I'll see if I can't smooth that out."

"Thank you," Rosey said. She gulped the rest of her water and rose. "I'll see you in an hour."

Atilio couldn't help but watch her walk out. That stretch-suit of hers left little to the imagination.

Though Atilio actually did have a good imagination, and had no problem at all imagining what was under that suit.

When he turned back, Moe gave him a huge grin.

"What?" Atilio had to ask.

"Nothing," Moe said. "Good luck, though."

Atilio deflated a little. He knew that Moe meant it, thought that he actually had a chance with Rosey.

Atilio knew better.

While Moe's luck tended to be good, Atilio's wasn't.

Besides, once they got *Aisha* back, he and Moe would be on their own. Looking for the next gig, something to bring in a chunk of cash.

His was a work-a-day existence.

And he had to be okay with that.

No matter what dreams he might have about someday.

FOUR

"Emma, darling! How are you?" Jamaal said, still playing the part of a gregarious merchant when he ran into his old handler.

He knew better than to think that this was a chance meeting, that Emma *just happened* to be in that particular hallway of the court when Jamaal finished handing Princess Jun Ogawa off to her minders.

This was one of the utilitarian parts of the building. More like an office space than part of the court. The walls were done in a color Jamaal thought of as government beige—designed to suck the life and interest out of those walking these hallways. Tough gray carpet covered the floor, resistant to stains. Even blood. Only a few flourishes made the area special, like the gold and green ribbons of color close to the ceiling, and the brass sconces with the symbol of the Empire embossed on the front of them—crossed katanas under a lotus blossom.

Jamaal wore a bright red robe today, decorated with white and black braid that no one knew was actually spidersilk, strong enough to deflect most knives. The robe covered him from neck to ankles, with enough volume that he could easily run, kick, or fight. The sleeves went down to his wrists, a bit tighter, but he still had full range of motion. Under his robe, he wore sharkskin armor. Not the full suit, not anymore. Hakeen, Jamaal's lover, had finally talked him out of that. Instead, it was a small suit, that only went down to his elbows and knees, while still covering his torso.

Maybe someday he'd go out without any armor. As he'd only been retired from being an assassin for the Emperor for about five years now, it wasn't time yet.

Hopefully, for Hakeen's sake, Jamaal would get there sooner rather than later.

Emma was dressed casually, in an off-white shirt that made her tanned skin look luscious, with tight black leggings that showed off all her muscles. Her black hair hung down to just past her shoulders—she'd either grown it out, or that was a wig.

Her piercing black eyes hadn't changed, and she effortlessly pinned him in place with just a glance.

"Jamaal, it's so good to see you!" Emma said, sounding as if she were surprised and not as if this had all been planned.

Probably had gamed out six different alternative paths, depending on his reaction.

Jamaal walked closer to Emma. "I've just arrived on planet, and I'll admit, I'm absolutely famished."

"Oh?" Emma said. "Anything in particular that you have in mind?"

"Well, there was that one hole-in-the-wall down on Shumanyi place. It served this divine steak salad," Jamaal said.

Interesting. Why did Emma grow slightly stiffer at that?

"Though I haven't been here since forever, and it might have closed. Or gone downhill. You know how it happens, nothing ever staying the same," Jamaal added lightly, giving Emma an out.

"While that sounds fabulous, there's this other place that I've kind of grown accustomed to," Emma said.

"Lead the way, darling," Jamaal said easily.

Only a few knew Emma's actual job—that of acting as the handler for various spies and assassins. Her supposedly real job was as a physical therapist.

"So how's the back?" Emma asked as they started walking out of the building of the court.

"Still doing my strength training exercise," Jamaal assured her. And he was. He regularly trained in his dojo, practicing one or another of the various martial arts that he'd picked up over the years.

They chatted easily about this and that, Jamaal filling her in on some of his travels, Emma complaining about the stupidity of some of her clients (without ever naming names, of course).

She did make one comment that struck Jamaal as interesting: "Of course, there's so much more to tell you. But now isn't the time."

"Of course, of course," Jamaal demurred, unsure of what she was referring to.

Emma led him down one of the main thoroughfares to a quiet back alley. As she maintained a casual demeanor, Jamaal tried not to get too tense or hyperaware, even in the confined space.

About halfway down, a small brass plaque next to a wooden door indicated that they had reached their destination: Morimoto's Fish Palace.

Jamaal was surprised that Emma had chosen one of the most exclusive restaurants in the city. Surely they couldn't just walk in and have a seat, could they?

It appeared that Emma could. The maître d was not expecting her, but still asked if she'd like to have her usual table.

The interior was designed like the inside of a conch shell, with low lighting and curving peach-and-white walls. Jamaal knew better than to send pictures of it to Dennis—Rosey might actually kill him if he did.

The maître d' brought them to a table on the edge of the room. A fountain sat between them and the curving wall, with white carp and turtles spitting out water up and down the four tiers.

It surprised Jamaal how loudly the water splashed beside them. However, he understood why Emma had chosen this restaurant, and in particular, this table.

It was probably one of the few public places where she could have delicate conversations in public without fear of being overheard.

As Jamaal listened, he noticed that the sound of the water changed now and again, as if tides pushed the fountain, at first, more water falling, then less.

It would be very difficult to scrub out a background noise that wasn't consistent.

Plus, he would bet that this "usual table" of Emma's also had some sort of privacy measures in place, capable of scrambling any trackers.

Then, there was also the fact that this was one of the most expensive, as well as exclusive, restaurants in the city. Anyone following Emma would have challenges getting a table. Even if they managed, they'd then have to spend an obscene amount of credits to eat.

Jamaal ordered the teacup soup and the sashimi special, letting the sushi chef choose his selection of fish.

Emma ordered a salmon-skin salad with a squid-ink pasta.

They both stuck to water. While Emma might be slightly comfortable here, neither of them were in a location where they could afford alcohol to slow their reactions.

"So tell me, Emma darling," Jamaal started with as the waiter left, "what job is it that you're trying to sweet talk me into?"

Emma glared at him. "You've changed," she said flatly.

"It's been five years. Of course, I've changed," Jamaal said. He found himself clinging to his trader persona despite the fact that he was facing his old handler.

Possibly he'd learned a bit more stubbornness along the way.

He'd have to let Rosey know that she was rubbing off on him. She was the most stubborn person he'd ever met.

Emma peered at him a bit longer, still stiff and unsmiling, before she finally relented. "Retirement's been good for you," she said softly.

"It has been," Jamaal said. "However, I remember my friends. And am here to help if they need me," he added softly.

Honestly, he wasn't certain how much he'd consider Emma a *friend*. He respected the hell out of her, and knew that she could kick his ass around the block without breaking a sweat.

He still had some remnants of *duty* tugging at him. Strings he'd have to cut one of these days.

"Prince Minato is very sick," Emma said after a bit. "It isn't well known."

It took Jamaal a few moments to place Prince Minato. There were so many princes and princesses to keep track of. "That's Princess Jun's brother, isn't it?"

"Yes, the middle sibling, the one who's actually in line to do something at the court," Emma said. "We have released press statements that he's slightly sick. Nothing about the full extent of his recent illness."

Jamaal nodded, encouraging Emma to go on. Official statements to the press generally bore only a slight resemblance to the truth.

Since the prince's illness wasn't new news, of course she felt comfortable talking with him out in public about it, especially in this semi-secured location.

When Emma finally realized that Jamaal wasn't about to say anything more, she continued. "We're not sure why he's sick. There's some speculation that it's poison."

That surprised Jamaal. How could someone get a poison to a person with such a high rank? Particularly given the high level of technology the royal family had access to?

"The family has actually employed an official taster, who runs all of Prince Minato's food through a scanner. He can't find anything that's poisoned. Even goes so far as to taste it himself. He doesn't get sick from it. But Prince Minato continues to remain ill," Emma said sounding frustrated. "And he's getting sicker."

"That's not good," Jamaal said slowly. "I assume you've accounted for all his other interactions?"

"We have," Emma said. "Which is why I argued that I re-activate you, so that you can start up an independent investigation."

Before Jamaal could protest, Emma rushed on. "You already have a connection with the family, through Princess Jun. You staying here can be easily explained by providing her with support during her brother's illness."

Jamaal nodded slowly. That was a good angle to take. Plus, he understood that the princess wouldn't be able to leave right away, not with her brother sick.

And he *had* promised to take her with him, when he returned to Niani, assuming that Rosey had been successful at stealing back the alien components.

All he was doing was biding his time until Rosey told him one way or the other about her mission.

"All right," Jamaal said. "I'll do it. I'll go visit Princess Jun this afternoon, see if I can garner any more details than what the family has already told you."

"You think they may be hiding something?" Emma said, her eyes narrowing.

Jamaal gave a gentle laugh. "No, I do not. They've been trained since birth to work with people like you, like Itsuki. However, they also don't know what they know. There's a chance that something they take for granted is the piece you're missing."

"Yes, that makes sense," Emma said. "Good. It's good to have you back."

Jamaal just gave her a smile, though inside, he went completely cold.

He was *not* "back." This was temporary. Another favor for a friend, as it were.

Meeting with Emma had just reconfirmed that he didn't want to be an assassin, or even just a spy, anymore.

This was a singular job. Period.

Then he was walking away again. Leaving it all behind.

Becoming Jamaal the trader in more than just name.

FIVE

"You're taking one of *my* flitters *where*?" Dennis said, breaking into the conversation. He hadn't just heard what he'd thought he heard, had he?

Rosey, Moe, Atilio and Ajax all sat around the dining nook. Dennis approved of that. It really was the most comfortable place on the ship. All his hard work acquiring the benches, getting the perfectly sized table, putting up what looked like brick walls painted over with white and pops of green ivy, had made it all so cozy.

Of course, with any decent sized budget, there was *so much more* he could do with the place. It really needed a bay window on one wall, with a simulated garden outside. Birds flying to and from a birdfeeder. And a fountain to add that essential sound element.

But alas, he'd had to make do with the credits Rosey allotted him and his projects.

Normally, Dennis only talked with the others when one of them directly spoke to him. It was something Rosey had insisted on. When it was just her, he could speak up at any point. However, when they had guests, he was supposed to be in listening mode.

No one, though, could blame him for demanding clarification about what he'd just heard.

The young man Ajax seemed a bit taken back by Dennis asking a question. Then again, that person was in far over his head, no matter how much of a bad-ass he thought himself.

According to the research Dennis had done, Ajax had been born to a good merchant family, raised in a rich and sheltered life. Then he'd turned into something of a black sheep, not following along with the family plans but trying his hand at speedracing.

Hermes 1 and *2* had both been speedships that he'd totaled during races. When he'd tried to get his family to buy him another speedship, they'd collectively turned their backs on him. He'd managed to leverage his trust fund so he had enough money to buy *Hermes 3.0*, but his family had refused to help him out anymore.

So Ajax had set up a "protection" racket, escorting ships in system. As there were actual pirates around, he had earned his keep. It was probably one of the reasons why *Hermes 3.0* was such a wreck, having survived being blasted at more than once.

That, and the fact that no one was paying Ajax enough money for a new ship.

Maybe this slight brush with fame would help his career.

If any of them survived the encounter on the planet.

"Did you just say that this Oswald's secret lair is on a volcano?" Dennis asked.

All right, so perhaps he was a little overly excited and it came out as more of a screech.

"Volcanic island, yeah," Ajax said.

"Like all the best super-villain lairs," Rosey commented dryly.

"Do you know what that volcanic ash will do to my engines? Let alone all the grit in the air filters?" Dennis demanded. "I still haven't gotten all the sand out of that flitter you took down to New Arrakis."

Rosey sighed. "It's just a flitter," she reminded him. Patiently. "It isn't as if I'm taking *you* planet-side."

The Roadrunner was a starship, with the shielding necessary for withstanding the rigors of hyperspace, not entry into an atmosphere and planetary gravity. Dennis had two flitters for doing the dirty work of going to a planet. *Hermes 3.0* was considered a spaceship, as it couldn't go into hyperspace and was meant for traveling in a single system. It, too, couldn't get down to a planet. Not without collapsing in on itself.

Which honestly, might not be the worst thing for that eyesore.

"I know you're only taking a flitter," Dennis said. He added a disdainful sniff. "But that flitter is then coming back up here and parking inside *The Roadrunner*."

"I'll help clean it out," Atilio said.

If Dennis could smile, he'd beam at the man. "*Thank you,*" he said emphatically. "Someone relies too much on inadequate robotic vacuums."

Not that he was implying that Rosey was lazy or anything. However, cleaning was her least favorite task. It was why so much of the ship was automated, both so that she wouldn't have to do the work and so she didn't have to hire other people to do it.

"Can we get back to planning how to take out an evil techno-wizard in his lair?" Rosey drawled.

"Where is the target physically located?" Atilio asked.

Dennis had of course investigated Atilio, as well as Moe. Seemed Atilio had a military background. He should be the one leading the excursion, not Rosey.

However, Dennis knew better than to suggest anything like that to Rosey. She had to be number one, in front of the pack, at all times.

Though this time, it might get her shot.

"The lair isn't actually underground," Ajax said, consulting his notes. "It's built into the side of a hill. The volcano is in the northern side of the island, while the lair is many miles away, on the southern edge, close to the water."

The young man looked up, tentative. Dennis had to hold himself back from recommending a new hair style—that floppy, greasy brown mane of his simply wasn't doing him any favors. Neither was the tough-boy black leather vest that he wore without a shirt. Even Dennis could see how badly it chaffed Ajax's skin.

And honestly, had Ajax thought that Rosey might be impressed by the scars he'd received when his ship had been attacked? The cuts on his arms or across his chest? Or those ridiculous tattoos? She was more likely to call him a fool for getting into a battle in the first place.

Really, the young man needed an entire make-over. Not that Dennis was volunteering for the job.

"Here," Rosey said, picking up the comm device that held Ajax's notes. She held it into the air. "Dennis, can you scan this?"

"Certainly," he said at the same time as Ajax said, "It's encoded."

Rosey just snorted at him.

Dennis had more than enough capacity (and experience, at this point) to easily bypass the security on the device and to read all the files. Honestly, he would have thought a pirate would know better than to allow his device to be open to all networks.

And Dennis didn't copy all the information on the device. He limited himself to just the stuff that was Oswald.

Really.

It took Dennis a few moments to get all the information in order and display the schematics of the lair up on the wall.

That hideaway, if you could call it that, was *so* gaudy. Totally lacking in curb appeal. Would make the top ten of the "worst designed" list for evil super-villain lairs.

Massive black doors blocked the front entrance, with atrocious gold steel bars looking like stripes running up and down them. The few windows looking out were black and reflective, like sunglasses meant to make someone look cool but just coming off as trying too hard. Gray steel made up the walls, probably reinforced and very protective, but showing such a lack of imagination. Vegetation was kept low to the ground, so no sneaking in through the bushes. The outer wall in front of the structure was just a shimmering lattice of lasers. Nothing was getting through that without being cut to pieces.

"A frontal attack probably isn't going to succeed," Atilio said, looking at the diagrams. "Those front doors are heavily reinforced. Going to be like a fortress."

"So no storming the castle?" Rosey asked.

"Probably not, no," Atilio said dryly.

"There's an inlet there, isn't there?" Moe said, pointing to the bottom edge.

Dennis magnified the place Moe was talking about.

"Think we could get there by going underwater? Through a sewage drain or something?" Moe asked.

"Ugh," both Rosey and Ajax replied simultaneously.

"No, it's probably guarded and monitored, if this guy is as much of a techno-wizard as you seem to think," Atilio said. "There's no back door either, as it's built into a mountain."

"I bet there is," Moe said after a few moments. "If he's that rich, he doesn't want food and supply deliveries going through those front gates. Those are to impress the *important people* coming to visit him. No, he'll have a side entrance for the peons."

"I bet you're right," Rosey said after a few moments. "Dennis, is there another entrance? On one of the sides?"

Dennis zoomed in. "Yes, the road from the front splits just after the laser fence. There's a much smaller road, not very well maintained, that runs around the perimeter to the left."

"Bet it leads right to the servant's entrance," Ajax said, nodding.

Dennis expanded that area of the front of the lair.

Bingo.

"And there's a landing pad right next to it, for drone deliveries," Atilio said with satisfaction.

"Thinking about making a special delivery?" Rosey asked.

Ugh. Was she actually flirting with this Atilio? Though Dennis thought more highly of Atilio than of Lloyd the Lounge Lizard, he wasn't certain he approved.

"You got it," Atilio said, nodding. "Though, there are beams located all along the top edge of the roof. Those are for shooting down any unexpected aircraft in the area."

And to make it look extra ugly. Dennis didn't bother saying that out loud, as he was certain the others were already thinking it.

Ajax said, "I could make some inquiries as to what sort of deliveries Oswald regularly has."

"You do that," Rosey said, nodding. "Dennis, think you could hijack an automated drone?"

"Please, darling. Of course I could. Wouldn't even have to worry about it taking any processing power. Unlike what it's going to take to clean my flitters if you land anywhere on that volcanic island. I can see it smoking!"

Really, did he deserve that much of an eyeroll? He did not.

The rest of the team continued to bat around ideas and make plans.

Dennis started looking up catalogs of cleaning supplies. Maybe he'd be able to talk Rosey into upgrading his entire cleaning system. Particularly if it was all automated.

After all, that was just ship maintenance, and should come out of *her* budget, not his.

SIX

Jun wasn't sure what to expect when she walked into Minato's bedroom. Minato was the only one of the three siblings to marry. She'd visited his home often, adored his wife Fumiko, as well as their two boys. However, the house had seemed hushed as she'd approached, like a dark shroud had been cast over it. The inside, too, was dark and gloomy, not at all like she remembered—overly ornate with knickknacks covering every surface, pictures on all the walls.

When they'd been growing up, Daiki had been the messiest of the three of them, his art projects spilling off of his desk, strewn across his floor, and covering every available surface. He'd tried his hand at many different types of art before finally falling in love with glass blowing.

Minato had been the cleanest, his bed always made, the books on his desk organized, even the trading cards and pendants from his current favorite sports team neatly put away. Jun had been somewhere between them, her primary failing being too many physical books scattered everywhere, as well as half a dozen tablets all holding additional reading materials.

The first thing that struck her was how dim the bedroom was. Minato loved the outdoors and lived with the windows open. The weather on Ishiman tended to be temperate, at least in the main city where the court was located. Even during the winter, when frost would kiss the grass, he'd stubbornly kept at least one of his windows cracked.

Now, not only was the room stuffy but overly warm. Light struggled to make it past the dark shades drawn halfway down the windows. Even with the fans kicked on high, the sour scent of sickness and musty sweat stubbornly clung to the air.

Instead of sports posters, the walls held portraits of the family, the two boys and their parents giggling and hugging each other. The room itself was tastefully decorated in shades of pink and peach, though the crown molding did have gold along the top and bottom of it. All the pieces of furniture had rounded corners, even the light sconces on the walls didn't have hard edges.

Jun was aware that they'd all grown up soft in some ways, hard in others. The gentleness implied by the decorations in here gave her the feeling that this had been a sanctuary for Minato, a place to retreat to, away from the world.

Medical equipment lurked around the edges of the hospital bed that had been brought in for her brother, replacing what had surely been a more comfortable bed for both him and his wife. The debris from his illness—pill bottles, syringes, medical tape and tissues—littered the end table.

Minato lay breathing shallowly on the bed, ashen from his illness, his normal tan washed out. His eyes opened as soon as Jun came up to the bed. At least they held some of his usual merriment.

"Must be bad if they got you to return from whatever dusty planet you were on," he croaked, his voice breaking.

"Naw, digging season was over. Had to stay some place when the storms came. May as well be here," Jun said, trying to keep her tone light.

That got her a familiar smile. "I'm still waiting for you to set the entire universe on fire with your latest discovery."

Jun snorted. "May have to wait a little longer." She didn't allow the anger she felt at Constantine to tint her voice, or to comment on her missing notes. "Seems *someone* got himself an owie."

"Wouldn't have been my list of things to do. Even if it did give me this grand vacation," Minato said. "I'll admit that for the first day or so, it was kind of nice to just relax and sleep in for a bit."

"Really?" Jun asked, surprised. Minato had always been athletic. If Daiki hadn't turned into an artist and had stayed with the court, Minato possibly would have pursued some sort of career in sports.

Minato shook his head. "I keep telling myself that. That this is just a nice vacation. But soon it'll be over and I'll be able to get up and go for a run."

"Yes, exactly," Jun said, nodding. "That's exactly what we're all waiting for. For you to get up off your lazy butt and do something."

"I'm trying," Minato said sincerely. He sighed. "But they don't know what's wrong with me."

"I thought it was some sort of poisoning," Jun said.

Minato nodded. "Yes. That's the initial diagnosis. But they can't figure out where the poison came from. Or why I keep getting sick. They keep cleaning my blood." He gestured toward the equipment on the far side of the bed. "And I'll be fine for a while. Then something sets me off again."

"I'm sure they've checked the food," Jun said slowly.

"They have. Even brought in a personal food tester for me. He scans everything. Even goes so far as to taste it before it's brought to me. But he hasn't had any ill effects. Only me."

"You'll kick this," Jun said fiercely. "If anyone can, you can."

Minato gave her a sad smile. "I have to. Can't leave my boys without a dad." He shook his head, shaking off the melancholy. "Besides, you'd personally find me in whatever afterlife I'd landed in and drag me back so that you didn't have to do the whole court thing."

Jun nodded. "You're right. Don't make me come after you."

She was a xenolinguist, a good one. There were too many things she wanted to do. Plus, too much of her work occurred off planet. She couldn't be tied to Ishiman, working as her family's representative in the court, and merely going through academic papers in the evenings.

Staying here would involve *politics.* While Jun had learned how to negotiate at a young age, knew many of the tricks involved with being an ambassador, as well as the important laws and treaties of the current age, she didn't enjoy it.

Minato looked at it as a game, like a competitive sport.

Jun would much rather deal with academic politics, where the players were much more vicious as well as less skilled. Though she honestly didn't care that much for them either.

"So I won't leave the current messes to you," Minato said.

"Promise?" Jun said.

Minato looked away, then said, "Could you hand me that water, please?"

A chill ran down Jun's spine as she reached for the glass, then held it for her brother. She thought about teasing him for using a sippy cup like his youngest son, but thought better of it when she saw his eyes.

The amusement had fled and all that remained was weariness.

They talked for just a few more moments before Minato faded further. Jun was certain that he'd fallen back asleep before she'd crept from the bedroom.

Someone had to be poisoning her brother. She wasn't sure how they were slipping it to him. He'd never been frail, never even really been sick when they'd been kids.

However, he wouldn't promise that he was getting better. He wouldn't lie to her, even now.

Which meant that he was possibly sicker than she'd realized, than anyone knew.

Jun was going to have to find out who was doing this to Minato.

And stop them.

Not just for her brother's sake, and the sake of his family, but for her own as well.

If Minato died, she'd never be free to pursue her academic dreams. To figure out what really happened to the Atoylee. To work on whatever new language or alien species that Humanity found.

Possibly, to ever see Moe again.

And that was truly unacceptable.

Fortunately, she had (she hoped!) a secret weapon, close at home.

Jamaal.

SEVEN

Duri Chang sat in her office on New Rome, telling herself to remain calm. Patient.

Serene, even.

When all she really felt like doing was screaming and tearing out her hair given the incompetence of those working for her.

However, she wouldn't allow herself to react that way, to give anyone who might be paying attention that satisfaction. The listening device planted on the underside of her desk would only hear her shuffling papers. Not much more.

She was a Director in the Kollective government, one of the highest levels of civil service available. Officially, she was in charge of the Search for Live Contact (SLC) department. Unofficially, Duri did whatever the hell it was that needed doing to push her agenda along.

Her small office reflected her rank in the Byzantine structure of the government, as opposed to the actual power her position wielded. The small room held a short credenza securing her less-than-important papers, a coat rack next to the door from which hung many coats and scarves, a mini-fridge that frequently had to be cleaned out due to the lunches she forgot to eat, and her plain wooden desk that was neat and clean, as always.

Duri put aside the tablet she'd been reading, paused to look out the window, and took a few deep breaths. She flipped a switch on her desk, indicating to her assistant Kiley to make her a cup of tea.

Kiley's ability to make perfect tea was one of the reasons why Duri kept Kiley around. Plus the fact that Kiley withstood Duri's recent storms without comment or cracking herself. She'd proven herself more than once in just a few short weeks.

So much so, that Duri had actually bothered learning her name.

Kiley slid into Duri's office silently, setting the teacup on Duri's desk without a word.

Duri nodded her thanks, then peered at the other woman for a few moments, pinning her in place, before saying, "Sit."

Kiley's brown eyes held the patience that Duri herself was missing that morning. Her assistant wore the slightest hint of makeup on her dark skin, her thick lips highlighted with a gentle pink that matched her professional-looking blouse. Pieces of gray, blue, and green hair had been braided into the multiple braids Kiley regularly had, cascading down her shoulders instead of pulled back into a large ponytail.

Duri made a point of never standing beside Kiley. Her assistant was possibly six feet tall and she loomed over Duri, who stood five feet two. Kiley was also curvy, while Duri was pencil-thin. Her aunts complained that she was skin-and-bones, and always tried to feed her when she bothered to go to the family gatherings on the weekends.

Only after Kiley was seated did Duri allow herself to stand and start pacing.

Kiley remained silent, not asking anything. They'd come to an understanding about these sorts of encounters, Duri explaining what she wanted, though Kiley had also managed to intuit a lot of what was expected from her before Duri said anything.

She really might have to hold onto Kiley for a while, unlike most of her assistants who generally only lasted a few months. If that.

"How would you go about seducing someone? Or at least bringing them to our side?" Duri abruptly asked, diving into the heart of her problem.

"Male, ma'am? Or female?" Kiley responded coolly.

That made Duri pause. Had that been her issue? That she hadn't considered the preferences of her target?

She paused, looking back at the notes on her tablet. No, this Lloyd Zachman preferred women to men.

Yet, he'd completely rejected the agent who she'd sent after him, the one with the goal of learning about his relationship with Rosey De Vries and why he was now experimenting with the chemicals and metals that had been located on the alien wreck.

The agent had admitted her failings, stating that Lloyd was completely faithful to Rosey, had even accused her of being a spy, though one sent by a competitor, trying to gain access to Rosey's speedship secrets.

There was nothing Duri could do about the agent as she'd been more of a mercenary than a high-powered spy. The contract hadn't had specific penalties for failure to deliver, which was reasonable for the sort of operation she'd set up.

Duri had still expected better results than what she'd received.

"Male," Duri said, "with what looks like a preference for females."

"Does he lack for female companionship?" Kiley asked. "Or does he have financial woes that could be exploited?"

"He's a well-respected chemical engineer, specializing in starship exteriors," Duri said. "So he's not hurting for money."

"No gambling issues? Or other unsavory habits?"

Duri shook her head. "Not that we've been able to discern. Does seek female companionship regularly, though."

"Does he hire professionals?" Kiley said after a few moments.

"He has, on occasion." That was how the original agent had been in contact with him.

"Do you need to keep him as a resource? Or can you burn him, once you have what you need?"

Ah, that was the problem that Duri was having. She'd been planning on developing this Lloyd as an asset, to get someone on the inside of De Vries' organization.

Maybe she could burn through him, arrange a meeting that turned into a sort of kidnapping, pump him dry of information and discard him, finding someone else later to embed.

If it was planned carefully enough, he'd just think he'd been rolled and wouldn't remember any of the questioning that had occurred.

"That might have to do," Duri admitted after a few moments. "I'll still need to find someone to embed in the De Vries organization, though."

Kiley nodded. Duri had told her enough of her plans for Rosey De Vries that Kiley could follow along.

Just then, a ping sounded loudly on Duri's tablet.

Duri stalked over to her desk and brought up the message.

Part of her frustration was that Rosey had yet to return to the space station *Lorenzo,* where she generally parked her starship *The Roadrunner.* But she'd been off station now for a few weeks.

Duri had still set up alarms for any mention of Rosey in any of the systems.

The news articles she saw perplexed her.

What the hell was Rosey De Vries doing out on the far end of the Allied Worlds' territory?

It didn't surprise Duri that Rosey had run—and won—a local race. She was that much of an attention seeker. She'd race anyone who challenged her.

Plus, she had no idea that Duri was focused on her.

Duri had been warned by General Carrick against trying to track Jamaal Akintola, or to set up repercussions for the man. Seemed that Jamaal was a former operative for the Emperor.

Having seen Jamaal (she was certain that he'd been the one to break into her house), she had no doubt that he was capable of extreme violence, if provoked.

She had no intention of triggering him.

So instead, she'd set plans in place for Jamaal's known companion, the person who'd broken into the facility on New Arrakis where the alien wreck had been housed.

Duri skimmed the first news article. It seemed that Rosey had run a race and beaten someone named Ronald "Ajax" Jackson, the black sheep of a prominent merchant family. He'd turned to piracy when his family had cut him off.

"New plan," Duri said abruptly as everything came together in her head.

Lloyd was too respectable to be bribed. Too well known in his community. Too certain of his place due to his education and wealth. He didn't have secrets that could possibly drain them away.

And he was far too loyal to Rosey.

This Ajax though...he could certainly be turned.

And Duri knew exactly which levers to pull in order to have her way.

EIGHT

Moe couldn't believe how gracefully Rosey landed the flitter they were in. They'd flown from *The Roadrunner* down to an island just south of the volcanic isle where Oswald was holed up. Moe hadn't even seen the opening Dennis had directed them to, just a solid canopy of exotic trees beneath them.

He'd bet that Rosey had maybe a foot clearance on all sides of the flitter.

Not only had she made it seem easy, she hadn't appeared to think anything of the landing. As if that sort of precision was just expected, not special.

Moe had always considered himself a good pilot.

He understood now that Rosey wasn't merely in a different league, but possibly a whole universe apart from where he stood.

"Here's our transport," Rosey told him as something pinged on her screen.

They'd had to time things perfectly—find the next load of supplies going to Oswald, hijack it, then replace the supplies with themselves without causing anyone to question the timing. They couldn't risk being detected. Oswald may have sensors on the adjacent islands, so they couldn't fly in and wait for a few hours.

No, all the steps had been set up with very little margin for error in the timeline.

Moe quickly slipped out of the expensive harness he'd been using while riding up in the helm with Rosey. At least he was back to his regular outfits instead of a stretchsuit—an oversized beige shirt, a vest with many, *many* pockets in it, cargo shorts, and sandals. The temperature aboard *The Roadrunner* had been a little chilly for him, so he'd been wearing thick black socks that Rosey had dug up for him, ignoring all the snide comments from Dennis about his style.

Or lack thereof.

The flitter, unlike *The Roadrunner*, had two seats up front, though Rosey hadn't needed a co-pilot. Despite her expertise, he'd found himself wanting to reach for the controls. He'd been a pilot for long enough that it felt wrong for someone else to be doing the flying.

Atilio and Ajax had been seated in the back. Atilio might be developing into something of a mentor for Ajax. As he'd said, he'd dealt with enough wet-behind-the-ears recruits in his time to know how to handle Ajax, even though the boy was supposedly in his thirties at this point.

At least Ajax had put away that ridiculous "pirate" outfit he'd been wearing and was now dressing in something that seemed more natural for him: a geeky dark gray T-shirt with an anime character that Moe didn't recognize, cargo pants with plenty of pockets, and armed to the teeth, like Atilio.

Rosey had originally objected to the number of weapons they were taking with them. Atilio had managed to convince her of the necessity.

Seemed that Jamaal had been the one who'd outfitted them with the weaponry.

Moe wasn't certain he wanted to know the entire story behind that, as she'd gritted her teeth and politely said, "I see," when Atilio had explained where he'd acquired enough guns to take down a small army.

Moe had his usual laser gun. Rosey had a couple of smaller guns strapped to her right hip and thigh. She also wore a baton on her left hip that expanded into a long, thick staff with the flick of a wrist.

He'd seen the dojo she had in *The Roadrunner*, was aware that she did a lot of martial arts. She and Atilio had sparred more than once during the few days they'd been waiting for the next supply run going to Oswald's island.

She'd joked about having developed her own weapon form, a wrench kata. As she wasn't likely to ever have a handy sword lying around for her to pick up and defend herself, learning how to wield a wrench made a lot more sense.

Particularly since after she'd mentioned it, Moe had realized that there were, indeed, wrenches stashed all over the ship. Not small ones, either. Big plumber's wrenches with heads as large as his two fists held together. Heavy, too.

While they'd been on the ship, Rosey had dressed in stretchsuits, but she'd changed for that day's sally, wearing a dark gray shirt, navy blue leggings that went down to her mid-calf, and ankle-high boots with a flexible sole to give her a better stance.

She looked formidable, not casual.

The four of them emerged from the flitter to find a small, five-foot square platform awaiting them. Spidersilk wires connected the corners of it to the drone angrily hovering above it, straining to get back up off the ground and to its allotted course.

Atilio and Ajax hurried over and removed a few of the boxes piled up on the platform, then waved the others over.

Moe looked at it with trepidation.

"Are you kidding me?" he said as he moved closer.

Did they really expect him to ride on a tiny platform for this island hop? There weren't any sides on the thing. No belts to strap themselves in with.

A good stiff breeze would knock them all off.

Rosey had already passed him, grabbing hold of the spider-silk wires on one side of the platform. Atilio and Ajax stood on the other two sides.

All three of those adrenaline junkies turned to look at him. Grinning.

Moe just sighed, shook his head, and took his place on the last side. He really wished he'd had a pair of gloves—the spider-silk wires were going to shred his palms, particularly given how tightly he was trying to hold on.

"It'll be fine, boss," Atilio, standing to his right, assured him.

Rosey gave a silent command to Dennis, up on *The Roadrunner*.

The drone rose sharply.

Moe gasped, his heart pounding.

Why was he doing this again?

At least the drone went straight up before it turned and headed toward the next island.

Moe kept his eyes steadily on the horizon. He was *not* going to look down at the endless blue water beneath him. Nor would he imagine the sea creatures that lived there, who would all find him a tasty morsel.

He tried not to stiffen up every time the platform swayed. He blamed the bright sun for the sweat that gathered across his shoulders. At least they didn't have to worry about the wind, as the drone didn't go that fast.

He still felt his stomach lurching more than once, leaving the sour taste of bile in his mouth.

The others shared maniacal grins, having the time of their lives on this ride.

Moe's only hope was to not die before they'd even started the mission.

Once they reached the next island, the drone took them down *fast*. It halted abruptly just a foot above the ground, then floated the rest of the way down.

Moe found himself shivering as he stepped backwards, off the platform. He shook his hands out and rolled his shoulders, rather than kneeling down and kissing the ground. As much as he might have wanted to.

"All right, what next?" Ajax asked.

The wall of the fortress beside them was featureless. A solid metallic gray. No handy finger- or foot-holds to climb up. No windows. No noticeable door, either.

Just then, a small opening appeared at the base of the wall, maybe two feet square. Out trundled a little robotic doll, with a large square head, wheels for legs, and retractable arms with four finger claws at the end. The head was actually a monitor. Currently it displayed white eyes, eyebrows and a little hook for a nose on its black screen.

Three identical robots scooted out behind the one. The opening closed as soon as the last one trundled out.

They rolled directly over to the platform, circling it, as if trying to come up with the best strategy for unloading the boxes.

Interesting. One braced itself, then a second rolled right up onto its shoulders. The third, then the fourth did the same, until there was a small stack of robots that was about the same height as the stack of boxes.

The top one reached out and grabbed the top box, handing it down the line to the ones beneath it. They quickly disassembled the box—evidently it had only looked like a single box, but was actually four boxes latched together.

Each robot then grabbed a box and rolled toward the wall. The small opening appeared only when the first one was a few inches away. It disappeared again as soon as they passed through.

"Well, crap," Rosey said.

Rosey, Atilio, and Ajax went to look at the wall. Probably wondering how to blow it up.

Moe ignored them, and went over to look at the boxes instead, to see how they were held together. He discovered two hooks on each side of the box.

"Does someone have a hammer? Wrench?" he asked the others.

Ajax wandered over and handed him a pair of needle-nose pliers. "These do?"

Moe nodded and went to work, attacking the hooks on the box. He managed to bend one down and twist it around so it wouldn't come undone easily.

"Want to explain, boss?" Atilio asked.

"There has to be a way to bring larger supplies into the building," Moe said as he bent a second hook. "The robots will work in concert to pick up the bigger box, and will open a larger door to haul it through."

"Smart," Rosey said, nodding.

"Make sure that you mostly stay out of the line of sight of

the robots, so that some automatic scanning program doesn't pick us up," Moe warned as the four little robots came back out of the stronghold.

They repeated the same performance as before, sliding up on top of one another, grabbing the next big box, handing it down.

Except that this time, they couldn't disassemble the box. It was stuck together.

Two of them picked it up, carrying the large box between them back to a different part of the featureless wall.

A person-sized opening appeared.

Moe and the others were ready, and slid through the door along with the robots.

The door behind them closed. The only lights came from the little robots as they trundled along at their feet.

Great. They'd made it inside.

Now what?

NINE

Jamaal had learned early on that those associated with the Emperor's court tended to go to one of two extremes in terms of their personal living quarters: either over the top opulence with everything gilded in pretty colors and no hard edges, or a quiet aestheticism with muted shades and very few possessions.

It didn't surprise him that Princess Jun Ogawa leaned toward the latter. Then again, this was only her home for part of the year. He'd been given to understand that most of the time, she preferred to be off-planet, either at a dig or doing research in some university library.

The air in the day room where he waited still held a touch of staleness from being empty for so long. A slight chill filled the area, and Jamaal was glad for his robes which regulated his temperature. Today he wore a muted gold, with more brown than yellow, though the robe itself was just as big as always, covering him completely. It went well with the couch he waited on, which was mostly made of wood with minimal white cushions on the seat and back. A second chair awaited the princess in the corner, a high-back affair with the same thin white pillows.

A sumi-e watercolor, painted on a large scroll that went from ceiling to floor, hung on the wall to his left. A skilled hand had done the work, though not a master. It showed a lone hut standing between a bamboo forest and a river, done in black and muted blue ink.

Had Daiki, Jun's older brother, painted it? Jamaal assumed so, as there was no bright red chop in the bottom corner, spelling out the artist's name in ancient characters.

It was the only decoration in the rather plain room. The floor was made from a light-colored wood, swept clean and polished but not reflective. Cream-colored paint covered the walls, warming the room. Traditional shoji doors, made from a dark wood with white paper between the squares, filled the far wall.

Opposite the painting was a window that revealed a rather colorful garden, full of flowers, with a fountain in the middle. Maybe it, too, could be counted as decoration, since it was a hologram. Though Jamaal doubted it had any real artistic value —Jun hadn't programmed it to show anything exotic, or even to stream something in real life. It showed the same birds and bees flitting from flower to fountain and back again, as if she couldn't be bothered to do anything more with it.

It probably doubled as a screen, letting her "visit" with long-distance guests. Or to have her attend something on the other side of the planet when she didn't want to go herself.

Finally, one of the shoji doors slid open and Princess Jun stepped through.

Jamaal was instantly on his feet, bowing his head.

"Princess Jun, it is an honor to serve you," Jamaal intoned, using the perfect amount of formality in his voice.

When he looked up, he was surprised at how formally dressed the princess was. She wore what was called a butterfly cloak, made out of a shimmering sky-blue material. Points on the shoulders of the outfit ascended far above her head. Loose streamers hung down on either side that flowed beautifully when she walked. The sleeves ended in hoops that made it difficult for her to drop her hands by her side. Though the top and the bottom of the coat blossomed out, the waist was drawn in, making Jun seem much larger than she actually was.

Hanging prominently in the center of her chest was a white bauble, her AI governess.

Jamaal was certain that Princess Jun wore some sort of sharkskin armor underneath the robes. The seams of the cloak, too, were probably protected by spidersilk.

It wasn't a very practical outfit. However, Princess Jun had likely trained from a young age to wear this sort of cloak with finesse and ease. She practically floated into the room.

"Jamaal, thank you so much for attending me today," Princess Jun said.

She raised her hand. Abruptly the window went black, as did the white bauble holding her AI. The walls hummed with power. A soft blue glow emanated from the baseboard.

"I've made this room as inaccessible as I can," Princess Jun told Jamaal. "Please feel free to verify."

Curious, Jamaal pulled out one of the scanners he always carried with him.

No trackers as far as his technology could detect. No listening devices, no recording equipment, nothing. Not anywhere in the room.

Jamaal looked up at Princess Jun. She stood motionless, completely serene, with her hands clasped in front of her.

He raised his eyebrows in question.

She gave him a faint smile and nodded.

Jamaal scanned the cloak of the princess, walking all the way around her.

Nothing. The AI had even been disconnected, which was an impressive feat.

As far as Jamaal could tell, they were completely alone, cut off from the rest of the world.

This didn't bode well.

He'd much rather be in a public place, like the restaurant Emma had taken him, then deal with such privacy. Particularly with an eligible female like Princess Jun.

If she made any accusations of him, it would strictly be her word against his.

"We don't have much time. Palace security will notice if I've gone offline for more than a few minutes," Princess Jun said.

Jamaal quirked an eyebrow at that. Interesting. So she'd done this before? When? And why?

"I'd like to hire you to find out who is poisoning my brother," Princess Jun said. She didn't bother sitting, but stayed exactly where she was.

Jamaal nodded, and returned to the place he'd been standing when she'd turned everything off.

When the lights and cameras came back on, they'd be in the same positions. That would help fool security into thinking it had just been a momentary glitch.

"Why do you think I can help do anything?" Jamaal asked. Though Emma had asked him already to help, he still needed to maintain his cover.

Didn't he?

Princess Jun peered closely at him. "You're more than you seem," she said quietly. "I don't need to know what your exact position is. I know that you have a lot of contacts, though, both inside as well as outside the palace. I need you to ask questions. Follow leads. Figure out who is poisoning my brother, and stop them."

"Not why?" Jamaal asked, curious. He would have thought that would be the most important question of all.

The smile Princess Jun gave him was surprisingly sad. "The why too, if you can. But there could be so many reasons why, so much intrigue going on. That might take too long to unravel. Finding whoever's responsible and stopping them is what's most important at this time."

Jamaal was impressed by the precision that Jun had given to thinking about the issue. Then again, she was an academic, and likely to be able to slice more sharply than Occam's razor.

"I will do my best," Jamaal said with a quick nod. "Do you have any suspicions?"

"It isn't constant," Jun said. "He appears to get better, then worse again. Which means that the poisoning is ongoing."

That wasn't something that Emma had mentioned, or knowledge that was generally available. Only someone going in and talking with the prince would be able to know that.

"Anything else?" Jamaal said. While it was something, it still wasn't much to go on.

"I'm certain that the staff have all been cleared," Jun said. "Probably multiple times. It has to be some outsider, somehow reaching in. Find where the hole is, Jamaal. And plug it."

With that, the princess waved her hand again. The blue lights around the baseboard of the of the room disappeared, along with the faint background humming sound. The window lit up with the same garden scene. Even the AI bauble hanging around Princess Jun's neck came back to life.

"Are you all right?" the AI governess asked.

"What do you mean?" Princess Jun said, looking around. "Of course I'm all right."

"Hrmph," said the AI.

"You'll have to excuse Sano," Princess Jun said. "She sometimes doesn't track things as well as she should."

"That's because you've only invested a sliver of my personality in this device," Sano replied. "I don't have access to everything I used to have."

"I will either get back the other version of you, and merge you, or I'll fully download you if that turns out to be impossible," Princess Jun promised her governess.

"Now, Jamaal, won't you please sit? I wanted to check in with you, see how your visit to Ishiman is turning out for you," Princess Jun said with a graceful gesture, indicating his chair. "As well as to thank you again for accompanying me here."

Jamaal gave her his best, sunniest smile and started talking about the various trade options that he'd located on this trip, as well as a truly colorful description of the dinner he'd enjoyed the night before.

Princess Jun entertained him graciously, offering bitter green tea with sweet lemon cookies that melted on his tongue.

All the while, Jamaal listened to everything she said, cataloging it, seeing if she would drop a few more hints as to what was really happening with Prince Minato.

And what exactly she thought Jamaal could do about it.

TEN

Rosey had read about villainous lairs. Watched ridiculous vids with maniacally cackling evil doers and their secret hideaway under a volcano.

She'd never actually expected to find herself here, on an island, with a *real smoking volcano* in the distance.

However, it made sense. If you're going to be that sort of evil technological wizard with a hidden lair, this was the place to do it. No matter how clichéd it might seem.

Rosey, Atilio, Moe, and Ajax had finally made it inside the lair and were now standing in the complete darkness, just on the other side of the door. Little robots carrying the only light source trundled away from them through the cavernous storage space.

Atilio had broken out a small flashlight so the group could see where they were. The robots had stopped in the distance, breaking apart the boxes, pulling out the supplies, scanning and sorting them, then rolling over and placing items on shelves.

Using her bonephone, Rosey made a call to Dennis, who

was still in orbit. She used the subvocal option, because she wanted to make as little noise as possible in this place.

Got any bio readings in here?

Negative. I can barely make out you four, Dennis replied sourly.

Rosey wasn't surprised that Dennis couldn't do a better scan of the building. He hadn't made much progress from orbit, and though he had access to everything Rosey saw, it hadn't really helped in terms of his scanning.

She was pleased that they could still be in contact. It meant that she might be able to use his lockpicking abilities.

If that didn't work, they'd end up using Atilio's firepower.

Rosey didn't approve of the group having that many guns. Weapons like that tended to make a person sloppy, to treat every problem as though it were a target, not a puzzle to be solved.

However, the fact that Jamaal had loaned them that much equipment meant he was expecting something bad. Oswald had been his contact back in the bad-old days when Jamaal did something other than just be a trader.

Got any ping on the ITT? she asked next.

Rosey had injected the alien electronics board with an intergalactic tracking tag, or ITT. She hadn't realized that Oswald had stolen the board until the ITT had started pinging her.

Nope, Dennis sighed. *Still just have the last reading from it, which is close to your location.*

The ITT had gone silent a day or so after it had woken up. Rosey figured that Oswald hadn't noticed when it had come on, or he would have silenced it immediately. She'd been able to track its movements to this planet. Then Oswald had moved the board into some sort of Faraday cage.

Had he noticed the ITT ping? Was that why he'd come here? Someplace where he could make a last stand?

Hopefully, the external security for his lair would make him lazy, and Rosey would find an edge.

She always did.

"Okay, we're going to go this way," she said quietly while walking forward. "Get to the place where the board was last pinging from. See if it's around there." Dennis had put up a map on the contact that she had in her right eye, that she generally read messages on.

"Lead on," Atilio replied. "I'll follow you. Moe, you're after me. Ajax, you're in the back, protecting our six. Got it?"

Rosey nodded. She knew that Atilio would much prefer to be out front, for any trap to have to go through him first. However, he didn't know where to go.

And this was still her operation. She'd listen to the experts, but she was going to lead.

Her place in any pack was always out front.

Fortunately, the door out of the storage area was people sized. How many people did Oswald have on staff here? Or was it all automated? Were there perhaps larger robots?

No noticeable alarms had gone off, though Rosey knew they didn't have much time before some automated system noticed something.

As they approached the door leading out of the storage area, it automatically slid to the side. The hallway was empty. It had the look of being "backstage," as it were.

This was where the servants and other peons passed. The walls were made from unpainted cinderblocks, gray and hard. Polished cement covered the floor. The air smelled musty and unused. Rosey would have a thing or two to say about the quality of

Oswald's air circulation system if they were to ever have a friendly chat. Canned lights in the ceiling gave the place a harshness. Again, meant for the little people, so they'd continue to feel unimportant.

Fortunately, the hallway led the direction the map wanted her to take. Dennis was quietly plotting and extrapolating where things went as Rosey walked along.

Left, Dennis directed her at the next intersection.

Rosey followed his instruction. They passed a few more closed doors, but no one came out to see the mice sneaking along.

Not yet.

Living quarters upstairs, Dennis said after a short while. *Laboratories and heavy equipment on this level. A few rooms beneath you.*

Rosey nodded. She assumed another escape route out from under the building, tunnels leading to the water.

Hopefully fully braced tunnels, if that volcano over there decided to blow.

The map on she could project from her left contact showed her that they were very close to the last place the board had been. While they strode down the back hallway, a parallel hallway was indicated to the right, probably where the important people walked.

Finally, they reached the location from which the last ping of the ITT had sounded.

As far as I can tell, you're at the back of one of the laboratories, Dennis told Rosey. *Look for a door.*

She quietly told the others what Dennis had conveyed. It was Moe who spotted the door.

Not a person-sized door, no.

A little robot door along the base of the wall.

"We need to get into what's probably a lab, on the other side of this wall," Rosey told the others. "Thoughts?"

"I can make us a door," Atilio suggested, holding up something that looked like an off-white dough.

Rosey didn't trust the manic edge that his eyes held. Still, they needed a way in.

While blowing an opening through a wall would certainly announce their presence, it would also give them the advantage of surprise.

Plus, Oswald's defenses were sure to be focused on the doors, not the walls.

Rosey gave Atilio a sharp nod.

He grinned and went to work, rolling the dough into long, thin strips and adhering them to the wall, as if the dough was some sort of putty. There was enough for a roughly three-foot high, two foot wide, door-like shape.

"Stand back," Atilio warned, waving everyone to the sides.

Atilio and Ajax got ready on either side of to-be door, with their guns out and ready. Rosey stood beside Atilio, and Moe next to Ajax. Moe pulled his laser out, looking undeniably the grimmest of the group. Rosey had a gun in one hand and had whipped out her baton and held it in her other hand, extending it to full length.

It wouldn't do much against a beam coming at her. However, it was a good distraction, and could also drive back an unsuspecting opponent who was too close.

Atilio held up five fingers, then counted down silently on them.

Rosey felt the explosion more than heard it, the force blowing all the debris into the room and not out to the corridor they stood in. She didn't know—or want to know—where Atilio had gotten military-grade explosives.

Jamaal? Or was it something that Atilio carried from his past?

A dust cloud puffed out at them. The hole was smaller than she'd expected—possibly smaller than Atilio had as well, as his face grew serious.

He bent over and rushed through the opening before the dust cleared, Ajax at his back.

Rosey took a deep breath, held it, and followed immediately after them, with Moe on her heels.

The light on the far side of the wall seemed grainy. It took her a moment to realize that was just the amount of dust and debris still floating.

While Atilio and Ajax concentrated their firepower on the robots who'd rushed them, Rosey took her time sighting and destroying every camera she saw perched in corners against the ceiling.

Ya never knew with those techno-wizards. Maybe some of those recording devices also came with lasers. A choice she was happy with when one of the "cameras" suddenly shot back at her.

Rosey dove when she saw it tracking her, executing a perfect somersault and coming back up shooting, destroying it while Moe took out another.

The battle was soon over. Rosey wouldn't say she was disappointed that she hadn't gotten to strike anyone with her staff.

No, really.

She was just glad no one was hurt.

Now that the firefight was over, Rosey could take the time to look around.

The room was very similar to the first lab Rosey had met Oswald in. At least a dozen long white tables filled the space, with various electronic gadgets in various stages of completion strewn across them.

All the little robots with big screens for heads had been destroyed. Seemed they came equipped with their own lasers that were powerful enough to shoot at people.

However, the place was empty. Oswald was nowhere to be seen.

Dennis? Rosey subvocalized.

No response.

The room they stood in blocked all external signals.

Rosey walked among the tables, looking for her alien electronic board.

There, on the far table. That looked like a stand that would hold an electronic board. Wires and alligator clips hung loose from the frame. Whatever had stood in the center of it was now gone.

"Do you think he knew we were coming?" Atilio asked, standing at her shoulder and acting like her own damned bodyguard.

Moe and Ajax were still shifting through the debris, seeing if they could find any clues.

Rosey shrugged. She had no idea.

She looked back toward the opening they'd come through, then back toward what looked like the front door to the room.

Something was off about the dimensions. When she'd had contact with Dennis, he'd shown her the parallel straight lines the hallways made.

The front of the room should be another three feet out.

It took Rosey a moment to realize that this room was *exactly* like the first room she'd met Oswald in.

The wall at the far end wasn't actually a wall holding cabinets. She strode forward, thrusting her staff into what looked like solid concrete blocks.

The image wavered and popped.

Oswald stood on the far side of the curtain, like the evil wizard he was.

He looked different than the last time Rosey had seen him. The brown hair had been a wig, as she'd surmised. Now, he was completely bald. Blue eyes glared at her, but instead of being piercing, they looked clouded. His lips were still thick, and the sneer was the same.

He was also considerably slimmer. Possibly down to a mere two hundred pounds. His dusty pants covered any cyber enhancements he may have had. His white T-shirt had also seen better days, stained under the arms as well as the front. It hung loosely on sagging skin.

Jamaal had said that Oswald didn't eat when he was mid-project, that he lived on all the fat he'd accumulated.

Those creepy metal spiders crawled around his neck, their stingers positioned to dive into him and give him, what, super strength? Super speed? The ability to fight his way out of here?

"You stole my property," Rosey said, her laser pointed directly at Oswald's chest.

While Atilio stood beside her, facing that threat, both Moe and Ajax kept their attention on the rest of the room, making sure they were safe, that no sneaky robots were rolling up to ambush them.

"It isn't your property," Oswald complained nasally. "This discovery belongs to all the people."

Rosey felt a slight twinge of guilt at that. She wouldn't be deterred, though.

"That's right," she said. "Which is why we stole it from The Kollective in the first place, bringing it to someone we thought we could trust, who could decipher it, so we could share the finding with the universe."

Oswald tilted his head to the side. "And get the credit for meeting these aliens," he accused her. "Having the first live contact."

Rosey shrugged. She knew that was part of Jamaal's plan.

More robots rushed in through the door. A few came in through the back. Rosey would bet that Oswald was talking with them, possibly subvocally controlling them.

Moe and Ajax handily shot every moving piece of equipment at it came through the door.

Rosey thwacked Oswald on the side of his thigh. Hard.

It wasn't enough to break a bone. It was still going to leave a good welt.

"Stop that," Rosey said. "Or I'll stop you."

Oswald's eyes grew wide and some of the cloud left them.

Had his eyes been partially blinded by schematics?

"You wouldn't!" he protested.

"Why wouldn't I?" Rosey said. "You're either going to deal fairly with us. Or I'm going to take this building apart brick by brick to find my property."

Oswald glared at her.

Rosey struck his other thigh, just for good measure, so he'd know she was serious.

He cried out in pain and surprise.

She didn't want to have to kill him.

Hopefully he wouldn't figure that out.

With a shudder, Oswald pointed to his left. It took Rosey a moment to realize that a curtain existed there, hiding the other side of the front of the room.

"The board and the data chip are over there," Oswald said, sounding resigned.

Rosey didn't take her eyes from Oswald. "If he twitches the wrong way, shoot him."

"Yes, sir," Atilio said with military sharpness.

Oswald's eyes grew a little wide at that.

No, *princess*, Rosey hadn't brought along amateurs.

Using her staff, Rosey struck the door that still stood between the two sides of the front of the room.

Huh. That was real.

Then she hit the far wall.

It disintegrated with a showy fall of sparks.

Two robots stood there. One was roughly man sized, holding the alien board. On a table beside it was another of the small robots with the large monitor for its head. It held the data chip. Another device sat on the table beside it.

Rosey didn't bother with them. Not yet. She immediately shot all along the edge of the ceiling.

Yup. There'd been a laser hidden up there as well.

At least the two robots didn't bother shooting at her.

Rosey dug out her comm and aimed it at the alien board.

It pinged right away. As it was in close proximity, it didn't need network access to assure her that the ITT was right there.

"So that's how you found me," she heard Oswald mutter behind her. "Clever."

Rosey just nodded and reached out her hand for the board.

The robot slowly, she would swear grudgingly, dropped it into her palm.

Before the robot could do anything else, Ajax shot it, frying it nicely. Sparks flew as it fell.

"What did you do that for?" Oswald demanded.

"No tricks," Atilio growled at him.

Oswald sighed. He nodded to himself, then he looked over at the other robot.

The smaller robot put the data chip on the table then stepped back.

Rosey swept up the chip as well as the device next to it.

"Thank you for building the reader that Jamaal asked you for," she said sweetly as she turned to face Oswald.

His face was a study in anger, blotches of red dotting his cheeks and sweat gleaming across his bald skull.

"You said I could have the board," he accused her. "As payment."

"I changed my mind," Rosey said smoothly. "I'll send you some credits."

Oswald tensed for a moment. Was that idiot actually going to try and attack her physically?

Then one of the AI-controlled spiders crawled out of the necklace circling his throat up to his cheek and jabbed him there.

Kinda rude.

Oswald shook his head and his eyes cleared all the way back to the piercing blue that Rosey remembered.

"Fine," he said. He paused. "I still would like access to whatever papers you publish."

Rosey nodded. She knew his type. He lived in the shadows, behind a desk, constantly vying for power among his small pool of evil super geniuses.

Maybe he could improve what she and the others discovered. When she decided to go public.

Hopefully, though, with these pieces, what they'd discovered would be actual, live aliens.

As if Oswald weren't alien enough, with his chemical system externally controlled.

"What now, sir?" Atilio said.

"He'll let us leave unharmed," Rosey assured them. "He

knows just how stupid it would be to attack. Because he doesn't want the cargo we're carrying damaged. Isn't that right, Oswald?"

Grimacing, Oswald nodded.

Atilio glanced at his laser, adjusted something, and stunned the poor bastard.

"Might give us less than a minute," she warned, given Oswald's enhanced system.

Then she stepped out the door, into the hallway. "You there?" she asked Dennis.

"I am!" he replied happily. "And I see you!"

"We need a quick exit route," Rosey told him.

A new map displayed on Rosey's contact, showing her the path to the front door of the lair. Luckily, they didn't have far to go, and Dennis had already dispatched a flitter to pick them up.

Rosey could tell that Atilio was disappointed that they didn't have to fight their way out.

Maybe next time.

When they went to confront this Constantine and rescue Moe's ship.

ELEVEN

Atilio walked into the back room of *The Roadrunner* where Moe was hanging out.

He looked as morose as ever.

Atilio contained his eyeroll—barely—and sat down next to Moe.

They were still in hyperspace, had been there for five hours and would remain there for another five.

Atilio didn't find hyperspace as disturbing as other people. Sure, the edges of the counters in here looked as though they were outlined in black, like some kind of cartoon. And his balance felt off. He did *not* want to try and work out, or do anything in the dojo. Potential injury lay that way lay.

But he could still walk around. Eat. Sleep. He knew some poor bastards who lost their lunch both entering as well as leaving hyperspace, and spent the entire time being space-sick. Wasn't much fun for anyone, as sometimes space-sickness acted like a really bad flu. For some soldiers, they started running at both ends.

Such happy memories he had of boot camp. Really.

Anyway, now he was here, on *The Roadrunner*. The back room wasn't as comfy as the kitchen area that Dennis had proudly redecorated. No, this room was more like a study, with large display screens more than one work bench. The constant scent of machine oil and solder had defeated even Dennis's filtration systems.

Or maybe he'd purposefully left the smells there, so that Rosey would feel more at home.

It was an amazing thing, to have such an automated ship. Atilio didn't know whether he should feel envious, awed, dismayed, or just thoughtful.

Possibly a combination of all of the above.

It was nice that he (or someone) didn't have to constantly be tweaking the engines. Though Rosey kind of did that anyway, making sure that she could eke out every ounce of speed from them. The shielding on the ship was far superior to any other civilian ship that Atilio had traveled on. He agreed with Rosey, though, to leave that cutting edge stuff for others, and be happy with materials that had proven themselves.

On the other hand, he wanted to be fiddling with *something*. Anything. He didn't read, not like Moe did—that lugubrious poetry that Moe preferred was a sure cure for insomnia, at least as far as Atilio was concerned.

He certainly didn't *mope*. Even if Rosey was so far out of his league. He could still stay in her orbit and bask from a distance.

All right, so maybe he was slightly mopey too.

Rosey had the data chip, the reader, and the board locked up tight in a secret compartment on the ship. She wasn't about to let anyone near them, not at this point. Not until they were out of Allied Worlds space and someplace that she considered civilized.

If they didn't know where the alien artifacts were, they couldn't tell someone if the ship got boarded.

Then came their next problem.

Actually walked into the room with them.

"Hey, guys," Ajax said as he sauntered in. At least he'd taken the hint and had stuck to the more geeky T-shirts and cargo pants, and not the faux-pirate gear.

Atilio didn't trust Ajax as far as he could throw him. Even though Atilio could probably bounce the punk off the nearest bulkhead without too much strain. Even in full gravity.

"Hey," Moe said easily.

Fortunately, though Moe trusted far too much, along with Rosey, Dennis at least had the good sense to be paranoid of the littlest pirate in their mix.

"Morning," Atilio said.

Ajax looked slightly confused. "I thought it was afternoon."

Atilio just shrugged. The first time you saw someone it was always morning, no matter the actual time of day.

And he'd successfully managed to avoid Ajax until just then.

"So, Rosey finally told me that we're heading to the planet Psykee," Ajax said. They'd been in general agreement to not talk about where they were going with Ajax until after they were already underway. Particularly as they waited the half-day for him to get his shit together on *Hermes 3.0*.

Atilio still wasn't completely sure why Rosey had agreed to let the boy tag along with them. He'd certainly begged and pleaded enough to travel with his idol. Even went so far as to threaten to just follow them.

As far as Atilio knew, you couldn't track someone through hyperspace.

Maybe Rosey had wanted the little flatterer around? Or she'd had a feeling about him? Keep friends close, enemies closer kind of thing?

All Atilio's gut told him was that he couldn't trust Ajax.

And maybe Ajax was part of the reason why no one except Rosey and Dennis knew where the alien parts were at this point.

"We are going to Psykee," Moe said in response to Ajax. "You ready for another fight?"

"I was born ready," Ajax boasted.

Atilio couldn't help but snort at the bragging youth.

Shit, when had he gotten to be old and cynical?

Probably before Ajax was born, quite frankly.

"What are we doing there?" Ajax asked.

Hadn't Rosey told him?

Maybe. Maybe not. Maybe he was just fishing for more information. Or maybe Rosey had figured that it was Moe's business, and left it up to him to tell the littlest pirate whatever he felt comfortable with.

"A warlord named Constantine," Moe replied. "And some unfinished business with him."

"Really?" Ajax said, his eyes grown almost comically wide. "Constantine? He's got a reputation as a badass."

Atilio nodded. "What can you tell us about him?"

Ajax suddenly grew sly. "Almost all his systems are manually operated, with a ridiculous redundancy factor. You know how you might put one guard on duty? And then someone on the outside might be able to bribe that one guard? Well, Constantine will have half a dozen, all jealous of one another. You can't get to all of them. One of them will turn against you. Plus state-of-the-art security for all his possessions. You aren't planning on robbing him or anything, right?"

Atilio knew that his grimace matched his boss's. They were kind of like an old married couple sometimes. More than one person had accused them of looking alike. Except that Moe continued to wear those ridiculous shorts, showing off dark brown skin and hairy knees with black socks and sandals, while at least Moe was dressed somewhat comfortably, in khaki pants with loops and pockets for tools and a regular shirt.

"Right?" Ajax asked again, glancing from one to the other of them.

"Well, kind of," Moe said. "I'm taking back my own property."

"On the planet? Or at one of the space-yards he uses?" Ajax asked.

"Space-yards?" Atilio asked.

"Sure. He has a couple of areas of space around Psykee that are marked as his. Kind of like junk yards, where he keeps ships he's taken. If there's a battle, he vacuums up *everything*. The hulls, the metal bits floating around, everything. It's like he's a bit obsessed with keeping the shipping lanes clean, you know?" Ajax said.

Atilio blinked, surprised. He hadn't known that.

Then again, it made sense that Constantine had some sort of space-yard, where he kept the ships that couldn't make it back to the surface, like *Aisha*.

"Where are these yards?" Atilio asked.

"I think I can get you the coordinates," Ajax said.

"No need," Dennis broke in. "I have just searched through the records and found them."

"Good work, Dennis," Atilio said.

Ajax looked slightly put out that he hadn't had the opportunity to reach out to his pirate network. Probably because it was a missed chance to brag about traveling with Rosey De Vries.

Or maybe because he wanted to sell the information about their plans to the highest bidder.

As if Dennis would allow Ajax to have any sort of private communications.

"Think you can locate *Aisha* by scans?" Atilio asked Dennis.

"Possibly," Dennis said. "I'd be working from size and shape of the ship alone, as I'm certain whatever transponder and licenses have been pulled and the ship has acquired a new identity."

"Maybe he hasn't touched her," Moe piped up. "Maybe he hasn't gotten around to dealing with her."

Atilio and Ajax shook their heads in tandem. "Not how it works, boss," Atilio said.

"No, you 'acquire' a ship, you need to deal with it fast," Ajax added. "Never know if it's got some sort of insurance or lien against it. Make it unidentifiable, so the bank can't come after you."

Atilio nodded. That was exactly how those sorts of spaceship and starship chop-shops worked. If a bank couldn't go after the existing owner, they'd go after whoever was in possession of the ship.

Atilio had received more than one job offer as a bank repo man. He'd turned them all down. He wanted not just to be able to sleep at night, but also to be able to look himself in the mirror in the morning.

"Though if the ship's too much bother, Constantine will just slag it," Ajax continued cheerfully.

Moe turned his big, morose eyes to Atilio. "He wouldn't do that to *Aisha*, would he?"

Atilio opened his mouth, then closed it again.

He was aware of what a junk heap the ship actually was. How everything had been patched not just once, but two or three times. How shoddy the shielding was. How the electrical system *really* needed to be ripped out and fully replaced. And the navigation system. And the exterior.

It probably wasn't even worth pulling the ship apart and trying to recycle the parts. Melting it down completely was probably the only way to get any value out of the thing.

However, Atilio wasn't about to point that out to Moe. Instead, he replied with, "Don't know, boss. Maybe. Maybe not."

Moe just sighed and continued to look morose.

"Maybe Constantine will sell your ship back to you," Ajax said, obviously trying to be helpful.

"No. Not at the cost to my soul," Moe said firmly. He took another deep breath then stood up, walking away. Probably going back to his cabin to wallow some more.

Atilio shook his head. There wasn't much he could do for Moe at this point.

Except be there to pick him up. To return the favor that Moe had done for him so many years ago.

To find Moe a new home, a new venture, a new direction, once this ride was over.

Ajax shrugged at Atilio. Atilio shrugged in return, then got up himself and wandered off, heading back to his own room on *The Roadrunner.*

Maybe Dennis had the latest issue of *Mechanics Illustrated,* or maybe he needed something fixed.

Or even cleaned.

Anything but to wait with idle hands.

TWELVE

Duri grimaced when she checked her budget numbers again. She wasn't going to go over the limits set for her. That wasn't possible. Not unless she wanted to lose her Directorship. The Kollective was very strict about budgets.

However, she was going to have to be careful for the next couple of months with her expenses. That little pirate brat had been pricey.

Fortunately, the promise to pay off most of his bank loans had finally been enough to get him to agree to betray his idol.

That pirate had waited until the credits had cleared the bank, then immediately transferred them to a second bank, so she couldn't reach back out and empty his account as quickly as she'd filled it.

Little sneak.

All of this had had to happen through a trusted Kollective agent, as there was no way to communicate immediately. Duri hated having to rely on other people's opinions, that this Ajax would give them the information she needed.

She'd had no choice in the matter. They'd had to move

quickly. All she'd been able to do was to give her counterpart a budget limit, never expecting her to max it out immediately.

Now, Duri waited for the first report to come from this new agent she'd just bought.

In the meanwhile, there was more paperwork to attend to.

As well as a meeting with General Carrick. Whatever could the man want now? He'd been rude enough to insist on another meeting in *person*, as well as in his office, not hers.

Duri had already promised not to go after Jamaal, this former spy of the Emperor's. And she'd kept her word. She hadn't even reached out to hear any back-channel chatter. Jamaal Akintola didn't exist as far as Duri was concerned.

So what did the general want?

At least he'd set up a proper appointment for her, through her assistant Kiley, instead of sending a nastygram email directly to her. She didn't know what dance Kiley had done with the General's people when scheduling the meeting, though she had the sense that Kiley, at any rate, felt as though she'd won that round.

If it became important, Duri knew that Kiley would inform her.

In the meanwhile, Duri got ready for her appointment by doing nothing at all. The general wouldn't be swayed by any window dressing.

She wore her standard "office chic" outfit, composed of a dark blue skirt and jacket, with a pale peach silk blouse that set off her slightly tanned skin beautifully. Her hair was pulled back on either side of her face with glittering clips that served as a distraction, nothing else.

There was no reason to apply more makeup. Nobody to impress with a fancier (or slinkier) dress. No way to gain the upper hand by preparing more reports.

No, Duri had to be enough with just who she was and what she knew.

Nothing else.

Fortunately, she was more than up for the task.

The walk that afternoon from her office in the administration buildings of the capitol complex to the military wing was pleasant enough. Summers on New Rome tended to be mild, though occasionally they'd have a hot and muggy day.

Despite it being well past noon, the air still felt crisp and smelled of the pines that grew beside the huge towers that stood guard outside the General Assembly buildings. While Duri could have taken one of the little carts that regularly wound their way from one seat of power to the next, the day was just too nice to be cooped up. Blue sky shone overhead, with the occasional glints of "invisible" drones, their shielding good but not perfect. Other government employees hurried in front or behind her, taking care of their own powerbases how they best saw fit.

The exterior of the military wing looked as austere as one might expect. Though all of the capitol buildings had been assembled at the same time, they looked completely different from one another. The military wing was solid brownish-red stone, with few details on the outside. Serious soldiers in serious armor strode along the rooftop. The windows were all heavily fortified. Two sets of gates had to be passed through to gain access.

Duri had perfected "inscrutable Asian charm" before she was a teenager. Nothing could ruffle her feathers, not even the interminable wait as the idiot at the front of the line had to go through the scanners once, twice, three times.

She suspected some of this was security theatre. The guards were watching the line more than the actor playing his part at the front of it. Was anyone suddenly nervous at the delay? Anxious? Looking ill-at-ease?

She went through without a problem, having learned her role early on.

The general didn't appear to have an appointment before hers, so even though Duri was early, she was still ushered into the stark office of the general.

No pictures livened up the small office. No rugs covered the hard wooden floor. Not even a clock dared tick its minutes away.

General Abdul Harim Carrick sat ramrod straight behind his desk. They'd never reached the stage where Duri had been granted permission to call him Abe. His richly dark skin with golden undertones showed his Arabic heritage. Silver fringed his once black hair, still buzzed short in a military cut. He glared at Duri from dark, piercing black eyes perched above a large nose and thin lips.

A few lone folders sat on one side of the general's desk. Duri glanced at them then away, interested in what new tidbit the general was going to share with her that day.

"What have you heard about Jamaal Akintola recently?" the general asked as Duri slid into the visitor's chair across from his desk.

She was certain that though it looked as plain as the rest of the office, it probably held detection devices able to monitor her heart rate, breath, and skin flush.

"Nothing, General," Duri replied truthfully. "You warned me to stay away from him. So I have."

"Hmm," the general grunted, pulling over one of the folders and opening it. "It appears that Jamaal may be more active than we once surmised. He's now on Ishiman, and has been meeting with his old handler."

Duri maintained a bland expression on her face, though she was fascinated by this.

Was Jamaal really a spy? Then why had he spent so much time (and money) on his Bigfoot hunt for aliens?

There wasn't anything more to those stupid hunters, was there? Some sort of conspiracy they had together that she should have seen or been aware of?

Duri foresaw spending a lot of time going over her notes of all those losers, looking to see if she'd overlooked something.

"He's also been seen in the company of Princess Jun Ogawa," the general intoned.

"Princess Jun Ogawa," Duri said slowly. Where did she know that name from?

It took her a few moments to put the pieces together.

"Sir, Princess Jun Ogawa is a relatively well-known xenolinguist," Duri said.

"I know that," the general said dismissively. Then he paused. "Wait. Do you think that Jamaal or one of those other idiots have finally found something truly alien?"

"You've seen my reports. Sir," Duri said, suspecting that the general had been lumping *her* in with *those idiots*. "I believe that the ship was destroyed en route to its laboratory was truly alien, and not of a race we were previously aware of."

The general sat back for a moment, thinking. "Jamaal doesn't have enough proof of the aliens to bring it to the attention of the Emperor? Does he?"

"I doubt it," Duri said.

"What do you think he's doing there?" the general asked, sitting forward again and spearing Duri with a piercing gaze.

"Possibly getting Princess Ogawa on his side, hiring her for work that will need to be done," Duri said. "There are other xenolinguists who he could reach out to," she admitted.

"However, he might have a personal relationship with the princess."

"I see," General Carrick said, nodding. He closed the folder he'd been looking at, then pulled out the next.

"One of my analysts was looking over the records on New Arrakis, where the wreck had been stored before being transported here," the general said slowly.

"All right," Duri said, nodding and maintaining a pleasant exterior, while cursing inside. She hadn't wanted him chasing down that lead.

"It appears that a known associate of Jamaal's, a Rosey De Vries, was at that location just before the wreck was transported here," the general continued.

He opened up the folder and slid it across the desk. There were two pictures on the first page. The first had been taken of Rosey many years before, when she'd still been a top-of-the-line speedship racer on the circuit. Her blonde curls were clipped tight to her scalp. She had a plain face, hazel-colored eyes, and pale white skin. Her grin sent chills down Duri's spine—Rosey was a wild one, for certain.

The second picture came from New Arrakis, as part of the false credentials she'd used. (Cameras in the area of the wreck had been working, but the data on them wasn't kept for longer than two days.) Here, Rosey was scowling into the camera. She looked much older, her hair a bit longer, the curls all gray. She'd not allowed herself to go to seed, though—her face was still thin and angular.

There was no doubt that the pictures were of the same woman.

"I'm aware of Rosey De Vries' association," Duri said slowly.

"Are you, now?" the general said, his voice nearly a purr. "And why didn't you think to inform my office of this?"

Duri snorted at him.

He looked affronted. Good. Men like him needed to be challenged more often.

"I'm expected to do your work, now?" Duri asked, not bothering to hide the derision. "My team had already discovered the things your team has. I had assumed that my team was reporting their findings to yours."

Was this simply a case of the left hand not knowing what the right hand was doing? Or was he merely trying to piss all over the investigation, to mark it as his own?

"Hmmm," General Carrick said as a reply, not bothering to make clear the cause of his displeasure.

He closed the folder and sat back, looking at Duri.

"I told you to stay away from Jamaal, which you did," he added quickly, before Duri could leap in. "You've been focusing on De Vries instead, haven't you?"

"I have been," Duri said. There was no point in lying to him. "But I haven't turned up anything to date."

"Brief me on what you have been doing," the general commanded.

Duri gave him a short account of the failure with the spy at the space station *Lorenzo*. It was even mostly complete and honest. No, really.

When she paused, the general asked, "So that's it? All you have to report is a failure?"

"No, sir," Duri said, trying not to show how peeved she was that she was going to have to report her most recent plans. She told him about the race near the planet Tyrone, that Rosey had won against Ronald "Ajax" Jackson.

And how Duri had turned this Ajax against his idol.

The general may have looked at her with something like respect for the first time.

"How much are you paying this Ajax?" he asked.

Fortunately, Duri was ready for that question. The number she quoted him was three times what she'd actually paid.

If General Carrick wanted to run this Ajax himself, the opportunity was going to cost him dearly.

It didn't surprise Duri that the general appeared to be considering it. However, in the end, he merely nodded and said, "You should stay in charge of this operation for now. Run your operative. But you need to keep me informed of any progress."

"I will," Duri promised easily, lying through her teeth.

It wasn't that she wouldn't update the general.

No, she would keep him apprised.

But only when she was damned good and ready.

General Carrick dismissed Duri after a few more exchanges. Duri decided to take one of the crawling little carts that traveled from one set of government buildings to the next to make her way back to her office. She didn't marvel at the day, or the warmth that had crept in, or even the sweetness of the breezes stirring her hair.

Instead, Duri planned, schemed, and put a few more resources into place.

She didn't know where Rosey was going.

Eventually, the ex-racer would return to the space station *Lorenzo*.

And Duri would be ready.

THIRTEEN

Jamaal checked, double-checked, then triple-checked all of the recordings for the food being taken in and out of Prince Minato's private residence.

He couldn't find any glitch in the system. No obvious places where the recordings looped in on themselves. No deep fakes done by a talented AI, showing what people expected to see and not what had actually gone on.

He'd even gone so far as to play all the recordings backwards, seeking a false trail.

There were none.

Jamaal sat back in the chair of the rental apartment Emma had acquired for him, stretching out his back. He hadn't had to spend so much time hunched over a chair doing research in quite some time.

Before, Jamaal had been looking at targets, acquiring openings that he could exploit to get closer to his assignment.

This meant he was good at finding holes in security.

However, this time, he was to block those holes, to stop someone else from using them.

Jamaal got up and stretched, going through a few of the arm-twirling poses of one of the forms of Tai Chi that he knew. He always called it the wing form, even though that wasn't its proper name. It just reminded him of that, given how often he swung his arms around.

The apartment was smaller than he was used to on a planet—smaller even than his rooms on *Lorenzo*. Space was sort of at a premium here, as he was in the capitol city on Ishiman, close to the court.

It was ample for his needs. The kitchen (unused, for the most part, except to make tea) was a small galley just inside the door. The desk and computer he used sat directly across from it. Then there was the single bedroom, with the bed that Hakeen would make fun of, given its size and relative lack of comfort.

Jamaal went into the tiny kitchen and prepared himself another cup of tea, using it as a sort of moving meditation while his mind processed what he'd learned.

No recent change in cooking staff. No one else getting sick. The medical reports showed a slow, insidious poison that hid in the bloodstream and was difficult to get at.

There had to be something that someone had overlooked.

Jamaal picked up his tea cup, then walked back to the desk.

For the first time in a long while, Jamaal wasn't paying attention to where he walked. The chair got in the way, and he accidentally kicked the roller at the base of the chair.

He cursed as he sloshed tea all over the cuff of his sleeve.

Damn it! Though there was a sanitizing closet that was adequate for his clothes, Jamaal didn't trust it for his more expensive robes.

However, it gave him pause.

Everyone *knew* Prince Minato was being poisoned.

Poison came from food.

Right?

Not necessarily.

Jamaal started tracking everything else that came into and left the house. All of the people as well.

Many of the servants had been with the family for years, their generations tied together. The Ogawas were mostly good people, at least as far as Jamaal could tell from the external record. They were generous with tips, with time off, with understanding that other people had families and obligations.

They were still royalty, and demanded a high level of service. However, they didn't appear to be assholes about it. (It was one of the puzzling things about this case—the Ogawa family was fairly well liked.)

Fumiko cooked often enough that food was regularly delivered to the house, instead of insisting that every meal be provided for them. Jamaal had had some suspicions about that at the start, but those faded after he tracked and retracked the wife.

No, Fumiko wasn't playing some long, desperate game, aiming to get rid of her husband and take all the power herself.

But did Fumiko do the laundry?

It took some time to track down the expenses of the household. There must be a washing machine and dryer on the premises as the family regularly bought detergent. Jamaal assumed that there was also more than one sanitizing closet, of a much higher quality than the one in this rental.

As far as Jamaal knew, there wasn't any way to turn sanitizing sonics of a cleansing closet deadly. Sure, that happened in extraordinary vids of super-spies who supposedly did the sort of thing that Jamaal did. Not in real life, though.

Jamaal was certain he was missing something. But what?

He laid down on his uncomfortable hotel bed and went back through everything Jun had told him about her visit to her brother.

Lights low. Shades drawn. Equipment surrounding the hospital bed. Prince Minato, pale. The smell of sickness. The feel of helplessness. The determination to do something.

Wait.

Jamaal went back through the details.

It was clever. Right in plain sight.

Now, all Jamaal had to do was to catch the culprit red-handed.

The driver of the laundry service was new.

Of course, he'd been vetted and background checks had been run on him.

Jamaal was far too familiar with how to fake those sorts of credentials. It wasn't that the watchguards had grown lazy. However, the driver was just another servant in some ways. He wasn't Important People.

Plus, he never came into direct contact with any of the royal family.

Jamaal followed the driver on his route. He made his rounds in a leisurely manner, no sense of urgency, though when Jamaal checked on the chat between the driver and his boss, he found all sorts of lies about traffic, construction, and emergencies, which was why the driver was almost always late.

Much more of that, and the driver would lose his position.

He didn't seem to care. His work history, what Jamaal could find of it, was spotty at best. He must have been being paid under the table frequently, doing jobs that weren't exactly on the up-and-up.

How he'd gotten this position was something of a mystery.

Still, the driver did do the work put in front of him. He would eventually finish his rounds and head back to headquarters for yet another batch.

His route varied, and he never visited the same house twice over the three days that Jamaal followed him. Jamaal timed the man as he stalked him, making sure that he understood the man's routine fully at every stop.

As Jamaal wasn't one hundred percent certain, he sent a message to Princess Jun that he was extending his stay at the capitol for one more day while he closed a particularly advantageous deal. Possibly, though, he'd be on his way after that.

At least the princess knew better than to demand that he visit her immediately, but instead, suggested that they should have tea again before he left.

On day four, the driver was headed back to Prince Minato's household.

Jamaal trailed close behind.

The driver parked in the driveway next to the house, having been waved through by the guards. Jamaal had stepped through the gate immediately afterward, having already acquired the correct pass for access from the princess.

So much easier than having to make up his own credentials!

He raced across the yard to the van, using a universal access fob to unlock it.

The door swung open.

The driver held the sanitized sheets and blankets provided by the hospital for the prince's bed in one hand.

And an aerosol sprayer in the other that he was using to coat the prince's bedding.

Jamaal didn't bother with asking questions first or getting the man to surrender peacefully. He stunned him immediately.

The driver fell to the floor of the van with a satisfying thunk, the aerosol sprayer clinking to the ground.

Jamaal didn't know what that sprayer contained, why the driver had been using it in the first place.

All he knew was that finally, he could get off this planet.

Go find Rosey. Figure out their next steps when it came to the aliens.

And go tracking after his true prey.

At last.

FOURTEEN

Princess Jun received Jamaal in her day rooms again. She liked meeting people there as the austerity suited her. It was also a good litmus test, helping her judge the character of those she met with. The people who fit into that clear space tended to make better allies, as opposed to those who either were uncomfortable with it or who commented on how poor her rooms seemed given her station.

In addition, she loved the watercolor on the wall done by her older brother. Certainly, there were finer works done by master craftsmen available to her. But Daiki had painted this one *for* her, for her birthday, years before. She often imagined herself in that little hut, with only the sound of the waterfall in the background.

That day, instead of the traditional butterfly cloak, she wore what was frequently called a medicine cloak, a garment that poofed out all around her body, made of emerald green. It was supposedly to keep other people from getting too close to her, to protect her from plagues and whatnot.

She'd rather rely on masks and modern filtration systems.

However, it was quite pretty, and she knew that later on that day, her mother would be pleased to see her in it. Particularly with the full warpaint on her face as well as her hands, to hide how tanned they'd gotten from all the archaeological work.

Jamaal was looking almost subdued in his dark brown robes, though the braid around the collar and cuffs was a brilliant white, and gold vines and leaves were embroidered across his chest.

"Thank you for coming to see me, today," Princess Jun said, graciously receiving her guest. They talked pleasantly of the weather, as well as Prince Minato's continued improvement.

"He's threatening to join one of his baseball games this weekend," Jun confided to Jamaal. "Though he really isn't well enough yet." The poison had finally been mostly drained from his body, now that it wasn't regularly being reintroduced. Plus, since the doctors now had a sample of the poison, they'd been able to make a much more targeted antidote.

"That's good to hear," Jamaal said with a smile. He'd asked to be kept out of the announcement of the discovery of the poisoner. "Palace security" received all the credit for the deed.

"So you might be wondering why I've asked you here," Princess Jun finally said as the tiny, delicate flower-shaped cookies disappeared.

"I was, actually," Jamaal said, playing along. He glanced around the room, but Jun hadn't cut them off from the rest of the world. Twice in one month, particularly when entertaining the same guest, would have caused eyebrows to rise.

"As you may recall, all the artifacts and notes from the dig on Niani were stolen by the warlord Constantine," Princess Jun said. She tried to keep the anger out of her voice, but knew that she'd probably failed. She just got too mad when thinking about all those artifacts going to the highest bidder, stored in some private collection, instead of being available to everyone. All the scientific work that would be lost.

"I do," Jamaal said. "I can make inquiries about it, if you'd like," he added. "I am planning on going back to that system."

"Good," Princess Jun said, nodding. "I'm going with you."

Jamaal gave her a tight smile. "Are you certain, my lady? Your family has just had an awful scare."

"I am," Jun said firmly.

It was true that her mother and father wouldn't be thrilled with her leaving again so soon. However, their son and true heir was recovering. He'd be joining them at court in the next week.

It was also true that she hadn't told her mother yet. That was this afternoon's task, and partly why she was so dressed up.

Not that she thought that she needed the medicinal cloak because her mother would throw a curse at her.

"All right," Jamaal said slowly, nodding. "I'll be finishing up my business in the next two days. I'll find us transportation at that point."

"No need," Jun said, waving her hand imperiously. "My starship has been returned from Niani. We can take that."

"I see," Jamaal said. "I appreciate the transport, my lady. But are you certain?"

Jun nearly rolled her eyes at him repeating himself. "I know that I will be safe in your company. Can you say the same about me staying here?"

After all, they still didn't know who'd hired the driver. It was likely to take some time to figure out his contact, as the man himself wasn't speaking.

Jamaal grimaced at that. "I cannot guarantee your safety. Constantine is a formidable warlord."

"I understand," Jun said. She really did.

Jamaal, like the others, would wrap her in cotton batting, trying to save her from the world as much as he could.

That would only stifle her, though.

She needed to be out there. Needed to touch the dirt. Needed to see what other aliens might be around. She hadn't forgotten what Jamaal had enticed her with originally.

"Very well," Jamaal said after a few moments. "I will still keep you as safe as I possibly can," he warned.

"I know," Jun said. "And I promise not to be too outrageous with my requests."

The look Jamaal gave her told her that her requests were already pushing the limit of what he was comfortable with.

"It will be fine," Jun assured him.

They made a few more plans before he took his leave. Jun allowed a servant to come in and take the empty serving trays away before shooing everyone away so she could just sit and think in her empty room for a bit.

Yes, she was going to have to leave Ishiman as a princess.

But it would be a young archaeologist who stepped off the ship at the other end of their journey.

A xenolinguist determined to get her work, and the work of her colleagues, back.

Even if she had to steal them herself.

FIFTEEN

Moe waited with Ajax and Atilio in the comfortable eating nook while Rosey went to get the alien artifacts.

When they'd first retrieved them from Oswald's lab, she'd put them into pouches hanging from her neck, then tucked them under the blouse she'd been wearing. She didn't bother showing them to the group until after they were well under way, not just leaving the current system, but after they'd traveled through hyperspace to the Psykee system.

Once they'd arrived there, they'd found a message from Jamaal, letting them know that he was on his way.

So they currently orbited one of the smaller moons of Psykee, waiting for him.

Moe wasn't sure who had begged Rosey enough to get her to show them her treasure, whether it had been Atilio or Ajax.

He'd also asked, but only once, and had easily taken, "Not yet," as an answer.

Rosey was back to wearing her regular, rose-colored stretchsuits, so she carried the alien parts in small metallic bags.

She held them carefully, like they really were some sort of treasure.

"One of the reasons I made y'all wait to see these was because I needed to make sure that Oswald hadn't done to me what I'd done to him, namely, inserting an ITT into the plastic of one of the pieces, or into the reader," Rosey explained as she came in. "These bags block any signal that the board or the reader may be casting."

"Dennis?" she said as she sat down, carefully placing the bags on the table.

"Standing by, boss," Dennis said.

Rosey slowly pulled a circuit board out from the first bag.

"Anything?" she asked, holding the board in one hand, ready to plunge it back into the bag.

"Nada," Dennis replied.

Rosey drew a breath and appeared to relax a little. "This was the first piece I found on the alien wreck." She handed it to Atilio, who was sitting on her right side.

He looked at the board, tracing some of the circuits, as well as scrutinizing the alien lettering. "I don't know of anyone who builds fiberoptics into their boards this way," he said, indicating a small bundle of fine gray wires.

"I know," Rosey said. "And I've confirmed that there are foreign metals as well as strange materials in the plastic, things we've never used."

Ajax glanced at the board when it was handed to him, examining the alien writing, before shrugging and passing it along to Moe.

The board was lightweight, with what looked like circuits and transistors soldered into it. It wasn't the standard green, gray, or black plastic that he was used to, but rather, a sky blue.

It was about six inches square and very light. One end of it was melted, probably where it had been attached to the alien wreck.

Though Moe was no expert, to him, the alien writing on the board looked similar to Old Norse, with the square, blocky letters. It wasn't a hieroglyphic language. The characters had obviously been stamped on, both on the board as well as a few of the circuits that stuck up from the base of the board.

There was no way of knowing what the board did. It wasn't bespoke, though. He'd bet that this board had been manufactured in large batches in some sort of factory.

Moe handed the board to Rosey and she put it back into the metallic bag. Only then did she pull out the other pieces, namely, the data chip and the reader that Oswald had built.

Again she paused, but Dennis piped up and said, "No transmissions detected."

The data chip caught everyone's attention. It glowed faintly, even in the bright light. It was about four inches long, three wide, and maybe a quarter-inch thick. It looked like it was made out of a durable plastic.

Rosey handed the chip around while she positioned the reader that Oswald had built on the table. It was about five inches long, maybe three wide, and sat another three inches tall. It looked fragile, with all the wiring and boards exposed. Two half-inch cables dangled from it.

While Atilio glanced at the chip then passed it on, Ajax seemed much more interested in it, running his fingers across it and examining both ends, before handing it reluctantly to Moe.

Moe couldn't help but shiver as the chip slid into his palm.

This was something truly alien. No one stored data on a glowing chip like this. The surface was completely smooth. "Where's the light coming from?" he asked.

"Don't know," Rosey said, obviously frustrated. "It doesn't radiate anything we can measure. But I'd bet it's internally powered. Somehow."

Moe handed Rosey the data chip. She picked up one of the cables and tried to attach it to the data chip.

Then she swore and turned the data chip over. Now, the plug went in neatly.

"There," she said. She fiddled with something on the reader.

Suddenly, a deep, guttural voice filled the nook.

Moe sat completely still as the alien said *something*. Followed by a second voice that spoke a single word.

Sentence. Word. Sentence. Same (???) word. Sentence. Pause. Sentence.

He was certain there were two voices. Two people talking about...something.

"My bet is that's someone running through a flight check list," Rosey said after a few moments. "Asking about the status of their ship and being told that it's okay, for the most part. Might be talking to a computer. Might be talking to flight control."

Shivers ran down Moe's spine.

Rosey picked up the other plug. "This is a standard data port. The reader Oswald built will output a phonetic transcript of everything that's spoken."

She paused and shook her head. "However, if this chip is like our own flight recorders, it will contain other data. Information about the vessel, the engines, and so on. The reader doesn't currently access those but hopefully we'll be able to figure out how to expand its parameters. Read all the data on the chip, and not just the audio files."

"Wow," Atilio said, his eyes wide.

Both Ajax and Moe nodded. This was amazing.

"The speaker that Oswald provided will produce sounds outside of Human hearing," Rosey said. "However, I believe that all the spoken language of the aliens is in our hearing range."

"So we might be able to communicate directly with them," Ajax said, "when we find them."

"If," Rosey answered, flipping off the reader.

"What about the rest of the ship? That these pieces came from?" Ajax asked.

"Some idiot blew it up," Rosey said.

Moe smiled at how angry she sounded. If she ever learned the identity of that idiot, they better be prepared.

"But it wasn't a ship," she warned. "It was a wreck. Complete shredded. Someone had flown it too long in hyperspace."

"So that means going to the system where the wreck was discovered probably won't do us much good," Atilio said slowly. "We wouldn't be able to trace where it came from."

"Exactly," Rosey said. "There might be more parts of this wreck floating around the area. Or maybe another ship. But it isn't our first stop along the way."

"Where are we going next?" Ajax asked.

Rosey smiled. "I think Jamaal will have the answer to that. And he'll be here shortly. With company," she added, throwing a glance at Moe.

Moe found himself swallowing hard against a suddenly dry throat.

Was Rosey implying that Princess Jun was traveling with Jamaal? He hadn't heard from her, hadn't received any sort of message.

What was she thinking? How was she feeling? Would she still respond kindly to him?

Or had going back to her home reminded her of just how hopeless any sort of relationship between them would be?

SIXTEEN

Dennis wasn't pouting. No, really. He was far more mature than that.

Just because Rosey had forbidden him from playing ceremonial music when the princess walked onto *The Roadrunner*. He had even picked out the perfect song, used only on special occasions in the court.

However, Rosey had said no.

To top it off, Rosey had also told him that he couldn't build a grand staircase as part of the entrance way.

Really. That woman just had *no* imagination.

Sure, it would have meant reconfiguring one of the airlocks. But he had it all figured out! The airlock would extend while the stairs unfolded. The current (inadequate) ship carrying the princess would just have to maneuver a little to stay attached.

It would have been beautiful. Majestic, even.

Spoilsport.

Dennis was determined to do something though, to

commemorate being a royal escort again. He hadn't had time to have the hallways reconfigured, to add gold crown molding to the interior.

He did have a monitor set up just inside the primary airlock. Instead of displaying bland ship information, or even the local news that Rosey liked, he put up the symbol of the Emperor, a pink lotus flower sitting on top of black, crossed katanas, over a field of gold and green, the colors of the Empire.

The Roadrunner was registered in the Empire. Wasn't it his *duty* as a loyal citizen to show the standard of the Empire?

At least Rosey didn't say anything when she saw it. She might have rolled her eyes excessively hard, but really, that was just Rosey.

"Greetings Princess Jun Ogawa! Herald of the Emperor!" Dennis called out as the princess and Jamaal stepped onto the ship.

Wait. Why wasn't she wearing one of her formal robes? She looked positively pedestrian in her plain shirt and trousers. Though that gray cloak of hers was fetching.

However, Princess Jun didn't disappoint. She straightened up, gaining more *stature* and *gravitas*, before giving a formal bow in the direction of the symbol.

When she stood up, she maintained a severe expression. "Dennis, correct?"

"Yes, your highness!" Dennis responded happily.

She'd remembered his name!

"Please, use the form *my lady*," the princess responded. "I am not the Crown Princess. I wouldn't want anyone to mistake my proper position."

"Understood, my lady," Dennis said. Oh, there was so much etiquette he was going to have to learn if he was going to continue to be a royal escort!

"At present, I am incognito," Princess Jun continued. "I am not Princess Jun Ogawa, but plain Jun Ogin. We are on a secret mission, and I wouldn't want to jeopardize that."

"A secret mission?" Dennis said. Why hadn't Rosey told him?

"Yes, I have been charged with recovering the alien artifacts stolen by the warlord Constantine," the princess—no, just Jun —said. "As we don't want to cause an incident between the Allied Worlds and the Empire, it must be a covert operation."

"Yes, I see," Dennis said, delighted. On the one hand, this mission did kinda bear a resemblance to the sorts of mischief that Rosey got up to regularly. On the other hand, this was *officially sanctioned* mischief! He might get a commendation from the Emperor himself!

Maybe he could get his registration officially changed so he could bear the standard of the princess.

"I am at your service. Let me know if there is anything that I can do to assist you," Dennis said immediately.

"Thank you, Dennis. I will remember that," Jun told him graciously.

Then she turned and smiled at Rosey and the others.

No, wait. She seemed to have the biggest smile for Moe.

Huh.

Rosey made the introduction of Ajax to the princess, who seemed properly awestruck that he was meeting royalty. Then Rosey herded everyone into the back game room. While the eating nook may seat four comfortably, six would be a stretch, unless they were really friendly with one another.

Jamaal insisted that Rosey show Jun the alien artifacts, the ones that Rosey had just stolen back, before they continued with their plans. Jun was fascinated by the artifacts and the recording. Dennis had thoroughly scanned the little reader that this Oswald had built, so was familiar with the schematics, as well as the rather crude interface that the man had built.

Rosey had tasked Dennis with figuring out how to improve the interface, to see if he could get more data out of the chip. She was certain it contained more than what they'd found so far.

Dennis wasn't ashamed to admit that he hadn't made much progress.

If the aliens had wanted a consult on how to properly arrange a comfortable sitting room, he'd be more than happy to oblige.

Digging around on an alien artifact while looking for more data?

Not his forte.

After his report, Jun asked, "Dennis, do you think that maybe you could work with Sano? She has a lot more experience with alien artifacts and languages."

Dennis had been aware of Sano from the start—that sliver of an AI that Jun had with her.

As she wasn't at her full abilities, Dennis hadn't done much more than send formal greetings and negotiate the small section of the ship that Sano had some control over, namely, the quarters of the princess.

Nothing more.

"I wouldn't mind an assistant," Dennis said, making it clear to Sano that she was inferior to him.

"I'm sure that will be fine," Jun assured him.

Sano, that stuck-up governess, at least had the good sense to agree.

The pair of them set up a separate channel to chat on while the Humans made their plans regarding getting back the ship as well as the containers.

Dennis had met other AIs who had more "physicality" as it were than he did. He never imagined himself as Human, never set himself up in a magnificent palace that changed with his every whim.

No, he was more outwardly focused, inhabiting *The Road-runner*. His "palace," where he kept a good portion of his consciousness, floated amid myriad colorful rivers of data. He had no form *per se*, no mass, just ribbons and streamers circling and encompassing him.

He had no form, yet every form.

Of course, Sano imagined herself differently. She was still a proper governess, and wore the formal, severe, peach-colored robes of her position. Her face was doll-like, more like a caricature than a Human's. Dennis didn't know if that was because she was so limited or if that was her natural look. She bore a faint resemblance to Jun, looking like an older aunt, with black eyes, a round-moon face, a small nose, and soft chin. She wore her black hair tied up strictly in a bun, with never a hair out of place.

The room she inhabited was bare of decorations. The walls were plain wood, as was the floor. She knelt before a low table and projected data on it.

Dennis sighed as he compressed himself down to occupy the same small space as Sano as he shared all the data he had so far, bringing it up on Sano's screen.

He himself dressed more like Jamaal, with flamboyant purple robes (though without the armor underneath), black hair and skin. He felt as though he was the one spot of color in all of Sano's world.

Except—now that he was seated on the other side of her table, he did spy a picture of Jun encased in a silver heart-shaped frame on the far wall. The princess was laughing, the sky was blue behind her, and joy emanated from the piece.

Dennis had his own embellishment—Rosey's initials embroidered on the chest of his robe, over his own heart, similar to what she had stitched onto her stretchsuits.

"Did Rosey mention that she thought the aliens might be left-handed?" Sano inquired after reviewing the data that Dennis had.

Dennis paused for a moment while he quickly reviewed everything Rosey had said about the aliens.

"She did," he said, recalling one of her initial conversations with Jamaal about it.

"Their language might flow from right to left, then, instead of from left to right," Sano pointed out. "It's easier to write that way, if you're left-handed."

"Huh," Dennis said. He hadn't even thought about how that difference may have affected everything in the physical world of the aliens.

"Which means that their code is also going to be 'left-handed' as it were," Sano said after a moment.

"Have you found something?" Dennis asked. He wasn't as excited about the aliens as Rosey was.

Though maybe, if he met them first, he could become not merely a royal escort, but an ambassadorial courier!

Just how far up in rank could he go?

And what would that do for his decorating budget?

"Maybe," Sano said. "It's going to take some time to break through. But it's why Oswald missed it. He was looking for right-handed clues, not left-handed."

Dennis had no idea what the other AI meant by that.

It didn't matter.

She was on the trail of something good.

While she worked, he could pursue more important paths.

Such as looking at the latest design catalogs (what Rosey referred to as his porn collection) and see what sorts of improvements he should make when he became an ambassador.

SEVENTEEN

Rosey checked her ID again.

Yup.

She was going to *kill* Jamaal when she had the chance.

He'd given her the name Rose "Atalanta" Jacobi.

Of course, she knew who Atalanta was—the Greek goddess of racing.

Middle names in this section of the Allied Worlds were customarily chosen from the name of a Greek god or goddess. Either the parents choose one, or the person picked something when they came of age. It was how Ajax had acquired his name.

"So what's your full name?" Rosey asked as she maneuvered the flitter down to the primary spaceport on Psykee. "The one Jamaal gave you?"

"June 'Psyche' Talisman," Jun said after a moment. "Why did he keep our first names? Or close to it?"

"That way you'll answer automatically. Even if they say it wrong," Rosey said. "It's why I'm merely a Rose, and your name's a different spelling. Makes it easier to remember that way."

"You've done this sort of thing before?" Jun asked, sounding a bit wary.

Rosey shrugged. "Not too often," she said. "And I've never stolen anything from a competitor. That would be wrong."

"Really?" Jun said.

"Really," Rosey said firmly. "If I can't beat them on my own, build speedships better than theirs, with my own smarts and ideas, then I deserve to be beaten."

"Huh," Jun said, obviously fascinated by the idea.

"Now, I won't say no to reading everything I can get my hands on about my competitors," Rosey said, warming to the subject. "There are always rumor mills to be found. Disgruntled employees who spill their guts, regardless of the NDAs they've signed. Watchlists of materials and metals that get purchased by companies, and speculation as to what they're building."

"Is the world of competitive racing that lucrative?" Jun said.

"It is," Rosey admitted. "I have Dennis, *The Roadrunner*, plus a large workshop on the space station *Lorenzo*. I own all of that free and clear. I have my own manufacturing equipment for making speedships. Fabrication units. Everything I need to take apart a ship and put it back together again. And I'm small fry."

"That's fascinating," Jun said. "I did go back and find one of your races to watch," she added.

"And?" Rosey asked, not sure what a complete outsider would think about a course.

"I had the option to watch the race as it happened in real

time, first, then to watch a slowed-down version of it," Jun said. She shook her head. "I don't see how you managed to move so quickly, to make all those minute adjustments to your ship while flying so fast!"

"Instincts," Rosey said. "And conditioning. And a whole lot of training. Why?" She had the feeling that the princess was leading up to something, but she wasn't sure what.

"Tell me about your training," Jun said.

So Rosey regaled the princess with stories of her martial arts training, the crazy teachers she'd learned from, even her "wrench kata."

"Weapons forms are the best for training your reflexes," Rosey said. They were nearing the spaceport, about to land. "Do you want me to show you the basics sometime?"

Jun gave her a grin. "I thought you'd never ask."

The bad news was as far as they could guesstimate, Constantine had already had an auction and sold the alien artifacts.

The good news was that all the containers appeared to be going to a single buyer.

The better news was that they were still to be delivered. They containers were still all located at Constantine's warehouse.

Rosey wasn't sure how she felt about educating a princess about a pigeon drop, or their equivalent of it. Probably wouldn't hurt for someone at her level to have a basic understanding of some sorts of crimes.

Hopefully she wouldn't then use that knowledge against anyone Rosey liked.

She had no problems with Jun (or anyone else) going against someone Rosey didn't like, or worse, didn't respect.

First item on the agenda—steal the transport vehicle, used to pick up the containers.

"You sure you're ready for this?" Rosey asked again as she armed herself with (yet another) stun gun. She had her telescoping baton attached to her left hip and an actual laser that could do serious damage attached to her right.

Jun nodded. She'd smeared a bit of grease across her forehead, the hood of her vehicle was propped open, and she looked hot and tired, her fancy outfit disheveled.

The road leading up to Constantine's estate was fairly private. Not many people came up this way. Trees hemmed in the edges of the asphalt. A cool breeze tickled the short hairs on Rosey's neck.

Rosey had placed a (small) explosive in the engine compartment of Jun's car, with a remote control that allowed her to set it off.

"I'm ready," Jun replied determinedly. "I want those papers. And artifacts. I'll do whatever I have to in order to retrieve them."

Rosey nodded, not saying anything.

Jun had surprised her. The girl was completely dedicated to the task.

To be fair—the princess wasn't as stubborn as Rosey. Few people were. But she'd definitely give the girl high marks in the category.

"All right, here comes our target," Rosey said, listening to the rumbling of a truck making its way up the hill. "You'll be fine."

Jun gave her a quick manic grin before worry replaced the expression.

Rosey nearly asked her what was the matter, but realized that was just Jun getting into her role.

It was showtime.

EIGHTEEN

Atilio sat at the table in the eating nook on *The Roadrunner* with Moe, Jamaal, and Ajax as they planned the rescue of *Aisha*.

Mostly, he stayed quiet and listened.

Though Rosey might believe Jamaal to be a simple trader, Atilio knew better. Particularly after the guy had outfitted them with top-of-the-line weapons and explosives for their excursion to see Oswald, stuff that the trader had just "happened" to have in stock nearby.

Though Atilio wasn't a betting man, he'd wager every credit he had (and some he'd have to borrow from someone) that Jamaal had been a spy for the Empire. Top level, too. There was a certain blankness to him. Despite the outrageous robes and outgoing personality, there were times when Jamaal forgot himself and *disappeared*, for want of a better term.

Turned into someone intensely silent and focused.

At those times, he reminded Atilio too much of the other spooks he'd met during his time in the military.

Jamaal was good. Ninety percent of the time, he wasn't *that guy*, and he acted in his usual jovial fashion.

When that stare returned, Atilio knew better than to draw attention to himself.

Like now.

Moe didn't know any better. Fortunately, Moe was merely naïve, and Jamaal appeared to recognize that. Moe had led a clean life. Mostly. Or clean enough. He was too small of a fish for Jamaal to be interested in.

Atilio's main concern was that Moe sighed too often over that princess of his. And Jamaal might not take too kindly to Moe's aspirations.

Ajax on the other hand...He was too young to recognize the shark in their midst. And he might become a tasty morsel for Jamaal if he wasn't careful.

Atilio would warn Moe about Jamaal. Later.

Ajax—he'd let be eaten.

Fortunately, Dennis appeared to have the same misgivings about Ajax, and had coded all the doors to not open for the boy. Fortunate for him, Ajax hadn't tried anything. Hadn't claimed to be "lost" and tried to go someplace he shouldn't.

Both Dennis and Atilio were keeping an eye on him.

And now, so was Jamaal.

"See, there's like a sphere of space-mines, all the way around the yard," Ajax explained. "The access points are right next to the generator and front office, as it were."

"Dennis?" Atilio asked quietly.

A hologram sprang up on the table, showing the space-yard in question. It was over a day's travel away from the planet of Psykee, if you were traveling regular speeds and using a regular spaceship. The image had bits of debris—parts, half-ships, and even engines—floating around in the sphere, with a solid, square space station in the center. The side closest to Jamaal had another square ship, looking sort of like a building. No, two buildings, one on either side of what Ajax described as the opening of the sphere.

"And where's *Aisha* again?" Atilio asked.

"She recently detached from the station in the center of the sphere," Dennis replied, "and been maneuvered to the back. There."

One of the floating pieces abruptly glowed bright blue.

"She's been attached to the station for the entire time we've been in system, so at least a week," Dennis continued.

That was a lot of space to cover: to get into the space-yard, board *Aisha*, then fly her out. If Atilio was reading the dimensions correctly, the sphere was about the size of a small moon. It couldn't be covered in seconds, or even a few minutes. More like an hour.

"Do you think Constantine placed her there on purpose?" Atilio asked after a moment. "Knowing that someone might try to mount a rescue mission?"

"Possibly," Jamaal said, nodding. "If I trusted that my security was good enough, I'd put her closer to the entranceway to make her more of a desirable target. Putting her back there means he might not be as certain about his security. Or he wasn't thinking in those terms, and just put her in the closest, most convenient spot."

"I would recommend coming in hot and hard," Ajax said. Again. "Blow up the two buildings at the front, drop the sphere. Then it's not so difficult to make it in and fly her out."

"Negative," Atilio said. "Those mines—can you expand the specs on those, please, Dennis?"

"Certainly," Dennis responded.

Atilio kept his smirk to himself. Ajax had asked—or rather, demanded—the display be shown earlier, and Dennis had ignored him. So Atilio was now going out of his way to be polite to Dennis.

Maybe the kid would catch a clue. You had to *ask* with a system as smart as Dennis.

Chances were, the littlest pirate wouldn't.

The specs of the three (three!) types of mines filled the space over the table.

Jamaal gave a low whistle. "Seems like a bit of overkill, don't you think?"

Atilio nodded. The generator at the front of the sphere only powered the largest of the three mines.

The other two types had their own explosive charge. They didn't need any additional boost to explode. All they needed was contact.

Illegal as hell. All three governments had agreed to that.

Allied Worlds, though, probably turned a blind eye when it came to some of their more powerful warlords.

The generator at the "front" of the yard probably also maintained the perfect sphere, regularly sending out commands to the mines to ensure that they were properly lined up.

If Atilio was designing this, he'd have a backup plan. If someone came in and did what Ajax wanted to do—namely, blow everything up—he'd have secondary programming that would send at least some of the mines flying directly to the front entrance. Sure, it would leave parts of the yard unde-fended. However, whoever had blown up those structures, when they entered the space-yard sphere, would be in for a world of hurt.

"I'm not sure that I want to burn that bridge so spectacularly," Jamaal said slowly. Then he then gave them a disarming grin. "Though blowing things up always has an appeal."

Ajax grinned in return, while Atilio just nodded.

"That structure in the center. That's the chop shop, right?" Atilio asked after a few moments.

"I'd assume so, yeah," Ajax said. "Easiest to place it there, equidistance from everything."

"Which means that *Aisha* has had some work done to her," Atilio said slowly.

"But that's good, right? I mean, they haven't slagged her," Ajax continued cheerfully, ignoring Moe's grimace. "Although...they might have just stripped her of all the good parts."

Atilio managed to control himself and didn't roll his eyes too hard at that.

Right. *Aisha had* no good parts. Honestly, she wasn't much better than slag. And even then, it might not be worth the effort sorting out what metals there were. Not unless you were desperate.

And Constantine didn't strike Atilio as desperate. Not in the least.

However, why had *Aisha* been attached to the chop shop for so long?

"Any other suggestions?" Jamaal said.

"Can we do a spacewalk through the mines?" Moe asked. "Slip in through the cracks, fire her up, then...I don't know. Then try to blast our way out?"

Atilio shook his head. *Aisha* didn't have any armaments to speak of. Just a couple small lasers to blow debris out of her path. Nothing to attack with.

And Moe knew that. He was just being desperate.

"Given the type of coverage the space mines have, I don't think that's possible," Dennis replied. He replaced the specs of the mines with the sphere again, then drilled down on one part of it.

"See? The mines aren't in a single array, but an overlapping pattern. While it would be possible for an expert in zero-G stealth operations to slip in, anyone else would need either cyber-enhancements to see the patterns of the mines as they shifted, or contact with an outside entity, such as myself, constantly feeding them information. And I'd be surprised if the mines weren't set up to raise an alarm if that sort of communication pattern occurred close to them," Dennis explained.

"Okay, so *Aisha* is in an area that's locked down pretty tightly," Jamaal said, nodding. "Maybe we do have to blow it open."

"See? That's what I'm talking about," Ajax said approvingly.

The group tossed around some ideas on logistics for a few minutes while Atilio sat in deep thought. Finally, he spoke up.

"Dennis? Are you sure that's *Aisha*?" he said when there was a lull in the conversation.

"Absolutely," Dennis said. "Her transponder replied to that name."

"Wait, so he hasn't changed her identity?" Moe asked, sounding as confused as Atilio felt.

"He hasn't," Dennis said. "Why would he? She's a perfectly fine operational ship."

"How good of a scan have you been able to do on her?" Atilio said, suddenly suspicious.

"Passive scanners only," Dennis admitted. "But I've had

them trained for a week on the location. So drips of information that have had to be assembled."

"Do you think he's been repairing her?" Moe said, hope filling his voice.

"That's exactly what he's been doing," Atilio said, finding only bleakness. "Don't you see, boss? If he fixed up *Aisha*, it would be yet another weight to hold over your head. Another reason why you'd sell your soul to him."

Wow. Atilio had never seen Moe angry before. Really angry.

His boss was one of the most easy-going individuals Atilio had ever met. He'd been upset, pissed off, before.

Not this level of mad.

Turned out that when Moe got *really* angry, he grew cold. Like, instant frostbite if you touched him.

Huh. Good to know.

Moe swore, invoking deities Atilio wasn't familiar with, as well as some physically improbable acts which may or may not have been blasphemous. (You could never tell with some of those gods.)

"We need to get her out of there. Now," Moe concluded.

Atilio nodded. "If they haven't messed too much with her programming, and if I can get a message to the ship, I could wake her up and point her in a direction."

"A remote call function?" Jamaal said, perking up.

"Yup," Atilio said, nodding.

Moe looked surprised.

Atilio was certain that he'd mentioned the fact that he'd built in a backdoor to the ship's systems.

Okay, maybe several backdoors, as he was never certain which program was likely to crap out at any time.

"Good, good," Jamaal said. His face took on a manic grin. "I know what we're going to do."

"Will it involve explosives?" Ajax asked hopefully.

"Oh, yes," Jamaal said. "Those will make a lovely distraction." He paused and gave them all a considered look.

"So, Moe," Jamaal finally said, "how do you feel about playing the part of a bored, pampered prince?"

NINETEEN

Jun stood in the middle of the road as the delivery truck came lumbering up the hill. They were well hidden from the fortress at the top, the curves in the road screening anyone from seeing them.

She waved her arms over her head, putting a distraught expression on her face.

Would they stop? Or would they swerve around her? She knew Rosey was prepared either way, having planted some sort of explosive up ahead.

Jun wore a colorful robe that she'd allowed to hang off one shoulder. Her hair was mussed, sticking up on one side, in what she hoped was a cute and disarming fashion, not crazed and wild.

She breathed a sigh of relief as the truck pulled up behind her "stalled" car.

Then she went rushing to the driver's side of the truck, yelling up at him.

"Oh, thank you, thank you for stopping! I was afraid I'd be stuck here all day!" she said, smiling up at the man. He was young, maybe in his twenties, and possibly a native given his Hellenic look with black curly hair and tanned skin. The man in the passenger seat was much older, and had been sitting too long in vehicles, his stomach extending well over his belt buckle. His once black hair had gone gray years before, and was in need of a good trim. And regular shampoo.

"What happened?" the older man asked.

"I don't know!" Jun exclaimed. "The engine started smoking and then everything stopped!" She held up her comm. "And of course, there's no reception out here in the middle of nowhere. I'm going to have to have words with Constantine about putting in some relay stations out along this road." She paused, then giggled. "Possibly even at my expense!"

Both men looked a little startled at that.

Really, boys. Those sorts of perks didn't cost that much. Sure, probably more than they'd make in a year. Or three. But not much for the likes of her. Or the part she was playing.

The driver sighed. "It's against the rules for us to give you a ride up to the compound," he said slowly, glancing at the other man, who gave a firm nod.

"No, that's fine," Jun said as she stepped back from the door. "Do you think you could take a look at the engine? I think it might need water. Or lubricant. Or something silly like that." She paused, looking at the car for a moment. "My driver has been out for the past month, and so I started driving myself on these little jaunts. It's been quite an adventure!"

At least both men merely nodded politely at that, instead of the eyeroll that she was certain Rosey would have given her.

"I'll take a look," the man in the passenger seat said.

"You could look, too," Jun said very quietly as the older man exited the car. She flashed him a smile. "That way, I can reward both of you for helping, instead of just *him*."

The younger man gave her a wide grin and nodded.

The pair of them followed her to the front of the car, peering into the engine compartment.

Jun stepped to the side, out of the line of fire as Rosey silently approached.

Without warning, Rosey shot both men in the back in rapid succession, stunning them so they crumpled to the ground.

It was over in seconds.

Jun still found her heart pounding hard in her chest. She'd only seen such things done in action movies. Never in real life. The palace guard kept such excitement far away from their royalty.

Rosey stepped closer and shot them each a second time, making sure they'd stay out for a while.

She nodded at Jun, then went to work, starting to strip off the men's uniforms to make it more difficult for them to leave once they awoke.

Jun shook her head, then her hands, trying to belay the chills running down her arms.

Then she joined in.

Jun had never stripped an unconscious man before. It wasn't as easy as they made it look in those action vids. The driver was floppy and difficult to maneuver, even though his uniform was a single coverall.

At least he wore normal, light-blue colored briefs.

The older guy, though...He had on white boxers with what appeared to be anatomically-correct hearts bleeding all over them.

Rosey didn't seem fazed at all. She tied the men up and locked them in the back of the car they'd rented (using a false ID, of course). The uniforms went into the trunk.

Watching Rosey hoist up the deadweight of one guy after the other made Jun appreciate just how physically strong Rosey was. When Jun had commented on it, Rosey waved it off. "These guys don't weigh anything, not compared to an engine."

After Rosey finished, she added, "Either they'll come to and rescue themselves, in, oh, half a day. Or someone else will stop and investigate what happened. As the pair of them aren't obvious, it will look like an abandoned car. Hopefully most people won't care enough to stop."

"I see," Jun said. At least they didn't have to put on the uniforms they'd stripped off the men, as Dennis had made matching outfits for them.

Though there had been quite a bit of complaining about how unstylish they were and couldn't he just add a bit of color, or even a dart here or there?

After less than five minutes, they were on their way up the hill to Constantine's compound.

Though Jun had gotten her emotions under control, she found her heart pounding again as they got closer to Constantine's compound. She, Moe, and Atilio had only managed to escape the first time due to the capriciousness of the warlord. Who'd then turned around and set up a bounty for their heads.

Hopefully, they wouldn't see him today. And he'd keep his mercurial nature to himself.

Rosey didn't go up the main drive, but followed a sign that directed deliveries down another road that went along the side of the large building, around to the back. They entered an area where the trees grew closer to the road, blocking off all sight of the building.

After they rounded a corner, the area opened up. As they

passed through the gap and well-maintained lawns surrounded them, Rosey suddenly spoke up.

"Okay. Just passed the first sentries."

"What? Were there people back there?" Jun asked. She looked out through the side mirror, but she didn't see anything except towering trees and road.

"Invisible gate that the responder in the truck automatically negotiated with," Rosey said. "If we'd tried to come up in a different delivery vehicle, we might have gotten a nasty shock."

"Oh," Jun said. Constantine really was paranoid, wasn't he?

Then again, he kind of did have reason to be.

The back of the building was still impressive, just not as imposing as the front. Not that she'd paid that much attention to it, what with the running away and all. A concrete, one-story structure stuck out from the rest of the tall, imposing building. At least half a dozen large doors filled one side of it.

"Garage," Rosey said with an unimpressed sniff. "Bet it's filled with supposed muscle cars that only look as though they go fast."

Jun just shrugged. She'd never raced, hadn't ever considered it a sport worth watching. Minato might know what Rosey was talking about.

"Is it a concern?" Jun asked.

"Naw, probably not. Though give me thirty minutes and I could ensure that none of those vehicles could ever catch up us," Rosey said with a grin. "This old jalopy has enough power to make her fast, with the right tweaks."

A man came out of the garage as they approached. He was dressed in a plain, off-white jumpsuit. Jun recognized it as a servant's outfit from the short amount of time she'd spent there. His bald head shone in the bright sunshine. He had an imperious nose that made it easy for him to look down at them. Given how little hair was on his head, he had a surprisingly luxurious black-and-gray beard that went halfway down his chest.

"You're late," he said as he walked over to the driver's side of the vehicle.

"Some asshole tried to stop us on the way up," Rosey said with a scowl as she passed the appropriate paperwork out the driver-side window.

"Hmm," the man said. "No one else should be up here."

Rosey just shrugged. "That's what we figured. So we just kept driving."

"Good," the man said, nodding.

The paperwork was all in order, as it was the original work order. Jamaal had said that recreating that would be more difficult than waylaying the truck. Jun wasn't sure why until the servant ran a scanner over the paperwork itself, not looking for an obvious identifying mark, but something woven into the paper itself.

"So where are the containers?" Rosey asked after the man handed the clipboard back.

"Door number three," the man said, gesturing to the line of garage doors. "Back up there."

"You got it," Rosey said as she put the vehicle into motion again.

Jun shot her an excited look.

"Not home free. Not yet," she said. "Just remember to be friendly and do your job."

"Yes, ma'am," Jun said meekly.

Rosey professionally backed the vehicle up as if she'd been driving this particular truck for years.

The door rolled open and Rosey backed up a touch more, keeping the cab of the truck on the outside while the rest of it was inside the garage. She climbed out, motioning for Jun to do the same, then stretched a bit, as if she'd been driving for hours.

Jun joined her and the servant on the far side of the vehicle. She wore a cap that they'd found in the truck to keep her face mostly hidden.

Rosey stood with her arms crossed over her chest, a slight scowl on her face.

"How long's this going to take?" she asked. "Don't want to screw up the rest of my deliveries today."

The man just smirked at her. "Then you should have gotten here earlier, shouldn't you?"

Rosey just glared at him.

An automated forklift scooped up the first of the containers, one of the original green ones, and loaded it onto the back of the truck. As far as Jun could tell, it hadn't been damaged, at least not on the outside. She'd have to inventory everything later.

She watched as the forklift trundled away, picking up the second of the containers. They were heavy enough that not even Rosey could have lifted one by herself, and they were awkwardly large—six foot cubes either in white or green.

The green ones held artifacts. The white ones held the papers from the dig.

Jun honestly couldn't say which ones she was more excited to see. Despite how much she valued the papers, she was also glad that the artifacts weren't going into private collections.

"Say, you look familiar," the guy said after a few moments of casting glances at Rosey.

Rosey shrugged. "Got one of those faces, you know?"

"No, that's not it. You look like someone famous. I know! That racer! De Vries," he said.

Rosey rolled her eyes at him.

Because Jun was expecting it, she also saw how Rosey adjusted her stance, ready to attack if the man put it together.

"What, is she your granddaughter or something?" the man asked, innocently.

Jun pressed her lips together to keep from laughing out loud.

"Cousin," Rosey growled out.

"Huh," the man said.

"And no, I can't get you an autograph. She's touchy about those sorts of things," Rosey continued.

"Just asking, no harm meant," the man said with a teasing smile.

One by one, the shipping containers were lifted onto the back of the truck, three on a side with a skinny aisle down the middle.

"That it?" Rosey asked the man as the last one was lifted up.

"It is," the man nodded.

"Let's go strap 'em down, then," Rosey said as she walked to the back of the truck and easily hoisted herself up.

Jun followed, though she wasn't anywhere near as graceful as Rosey getting up into the vehicle.

Rosey shook her head and caught the eye of the servant. "Kids these days. Gotta teach 'em everything."

The older man gave them a big grin.

Rosey walked down the aisle formed by the two rows of containers, then handed Jun a set of long straps with hooks on either end.

"Connect one end to the front of the truck, walk down,

building yourself a single strap, and connect the last one to the wall down there. Got it?" Rosey said.

"I'm not twelve, you know," Jun whined. "I've done this before." Though she hadn't. She was just playing her part of the new kid.

"Right," Rosey replied, the sarcasm thick enough to cloud the air.

She stood with her arms crossed over her chest as Jun went ahead and did as Rosey asked, the eyes of the servant on them the entire time.

When Jun finished with her side, Rosey handed her the rest of the straps to do the other side while Rosey attached a cinch and tightened up the first set of straps.

Jun already had a clue how strong Rosey was. That she managed to tighten the straps enough to draw the containers closer to one another was impressive.

Once they were finished, Rosey carelessly signed the paperwork that the man handed her. He checked her signature against the ID she carried, that Jamaal had given them, then nodded them on their way.

It wasn't until after they'd gotten past the open area, back into the woods, that Jun finally gave Rosey an excited smile.

"We did it!" she exclaimed.

"Don't get cocky. I don't trust a job being finished until after everything's back under my full control," Rosey warned. "That means on *The Roadrunner*."

Jun nodded and subsided. A little.

They'd managed to steal back all the missing containers.

Now, hopefully, she and Moe could deliver them to their rightful location on *Aisha*.

TWENTY

Jamaal wouldn't admit it to anyone. Certainly not to this crew. Maybe to Rosey after they'd had enough to drink. Or perhaps Harkeen.

But Jamaal was having *fun*.

He'd never enjoyed being a spy all that much. There had always been too much pressure to perform well, to accomplish his mission. He'd always had a sense of tremendous satisfaction once he'd finished an assignment, but that was always after the fact.

If things didn't go well here, there would be consequences. He might even end up shooting his way in, then out.

A mass casualty incident was the mark of an amateur. Which was why he was loathe to do it. Unlike Ajax, who'd seemed particularly disappointed that he wasn't going to have the chance to blow up everything.

A few minor explosions would hopefully soothe the poor boy's soul.

Moe walked next to him as they exited the flitter and

entered the front-office ship of the space-yard. He looked sparkly, for want of a better word.

Jamaal had given Dennis free rein when it came to generating a costume for Moe. Maybe that had been a mistake. Jamaal at his most exuberant would never match what Moe was currently wearing. Probably.

The good news, though, was that Moe wore the outfit (instead of the outfit wearing him) and managed to carry it off well.

To start off with, the turban was completely impractical in space, piled up high on Moe's head, made from wound layers of silver cloth with gold embroidery. The jacket—a *sherwani*, as Dennis had stuffily corrected him—was made from similar material. It emphasized Moe's shoulders and was pulled in tightly at the waist, falling down to mid-thigh.

Again, totally impractical if there was an emergency and you needed to don a spacesuit. Though maybe under all those layers, Moe could wear a stretchsuit.

Underneath the jacket were mostly white pants. The only decoration on those was a band of gold down the outside seams. As well as the sparkling material that the pants were made of.

Instead of Moe's usual sandals, he wore what looked like black velvet slippers, complete with little points on the toes that somehow didn't look completely ridiculous.

In fact...they actually looked pretty comfortable. Jamaal might ask Dennis to whip him up something similar. As long as the toes could still be reinforced with steel.

The guards at the front of the station had taken one look at Moe and Jamaal, who looked positively *dowdy* in a plain brown robe with gold embroidery, and decided that this matter was far above their pay grade. Instead of stopping them, they immediately directed them to the office of the station manager. The name on the door said *Ellis Hawkings.*

"Where is my ship?" Moe demanded haughtily upon *sweeping* into the office.

It was a rather dismal place, barely big enough for the manager and his sparse furniture. A long shop light in the ceiling shown down harshly on the desk piled with papers. The handheld comm on the side was ancient and clunky, made of cracked black plastic. An equally ancient monitor was set up on the desk, partially blocked by rows of notes stuck to it. The air stank of engine oil, cheap fried food, and failed dreams.

Jamaal flowed to Moe's side. "Please, my prince, let me try to handle this first."

Moe glowered at Jamaal but then subsided. "Very well. Prove your worth to me yet again. If you can," he said, taking a step back.

"Constantine has promised Prince Tennakoon a ship from this yard after losing at a certain game of chance," Jamaal told Ellis.

"He didn't lose," Moe muttered darkly. "He cheated and I caught him. Very sloppy."

"Indeed, my prince," Jamaal said. He turned back to Ellis and rolled his eyes subtly, a blatant attempt to get the man on his side.

It appeared to work, as the man suppressed a smile, then nodded at Jamaal to continue.

"Constantine has a new ship that he's been reoutfitting, correct?" Jamaal said, reeling off the call letters for *Aisha.* "We understand that most of the work is done?"

Ellis started up his old computer and had Jamaal repeat the numbers.

Jamaal was surprised that the smell of burning wires didn't

fill the small space as, from the sound of it, the fan of the computer was already working overtime.

Give it a while.

"Yes, it's here," Ellis said with a frown. "But only the exterior has been updated. New shielding, newish engines. Nothing's been done to the interior."

"Exactly," Moe said regally. "I would never trust Constantine to provide the elegance that my stature requires."

Jamaal shut his eyes for just a moment and gave a minute shake of his head. When he opened them again, he gave Ellis a sheepish grin. "So that's the ship," Jamaal said. "We need to acquire it now."

"Give him the bill of sale. Or whatever it was that Constantine called it," Moe directed.

"I only have an electronic version," Jamaal said sheepishly. "Where can I send it?"

Ellis slowly shook his head. "No. Constantine deals with paper. Only."

Jamaal nodded. He'd already known that, based on what records Dennis had been able to scrounge. "I know. I understand. These are special circumstances, though." He cast a quick glance over his shoulder at Moe, trying to give the impression that he was nervous.

Moe stood, drawn up to his full height, arms crossed high over his chest, literally looking down his nose at the pair of them.

Jamaal was tall, just a hair over six feet tall. It was easy to forget that Moe was taller, given the way the man normally carried himself.

"Due to the circumstances under which we find ourselves in possession of this ship, we thought it was expedient to claim her now. Rather than wait for Constantine to go back on his word. Again," Moe thundered.

Ellis looked wary. Seemed he was a bit more afraid of his boss than of the irate prince standing in his office.

"Please," Jamaal whined. "I'm sure the prince would be *very* willing to show his gratitude if you expedited this matter."

At least Ellis perked up at that.

"Take it out of the usual fund," Moe said airily, as if he were used to paying bribes.

"Uhm, can I see that bill of sale? On your comm?" Ellis asked.

"Certainly," Jamaal said, drawing out his own comm and calling up the bill of sale that he'd meticulously pieced together.

"It looks authentic," Ellis said grumbled.

Moe merely sent him a glare that would have frozen a lesser being into a solid chunk of ice.

"I'm sorry," Ellis said. "It really—"

A loud alarm suddenly sounded.

"Don't tell me that this station has been breached," Moe said, sounding murderous.

"No, no, that isn't it," Ellis assured them both. He sat, his attention glued to his screen as he toggled furiously. "Someone is trying to cross the perimeter."

"I would hope that Constantine has more than enough automated systems to handle such a clumsy attempt," Moe said frostily.

"He does," Ellis said, sitting back and taking a quick breath. He glanced at Jamaal, then at Moe, and realized that the only way out of his office meant going through both of them.

"Of course, you could always make it look as though those

systems failed, which is why the ship is no longer here," Jamaal suggested.

Ellis nodded thoughtfully. "That's a possibility."

A second set of alarms suddenly went off and Ellis just shook his head. "The ship—oh. The ship is already almost here."

"See, my prince? Constantine wasn't going back on his word that he'd have the ship ready for you, waiting by the entrance of the space-yard."

"He better," Moe growled.

"So if we could continue?" Jamaal asked.

It took just a few more fake signatures for the deed to be transferred.

"Thank you," Jamaal said as he pressed a credit stick into Ellis's hands before he bowed his way out.

There weren't that many credits on the stick. Jamaal wasn't about to bankrupt himself on this venture.

Still, hopefully it would make up for whatever Constantine would throw at the man for losing *Aisha*.

TWENTY-ONE

Moe stood in the cockpit of *Aisha*, behind the pilot's seat, feeling himself settle.

While much of the interior of the ship remained the same, there were noticeable differences as well.

First of all, the smells were different. Someone had replaced the air filters—possibly the entire air filtration system—so everything smelled fresher, now.

The engines, too, had been replaced. Not with brand-new, top-of-the-line equipment, but at least a couple of generations better than what *Aisha* had been equipped with. As had the shielding, which meant that they could spend a lot longer in hyperspace and not have to bounce out every few hours.

They'd also replaced the pilot's control panel. The new one looked ugly, a bright silver monstrosity roughly shoved into a smaller space that had once looked quaint. Rosey had muttered something about a hack job, and was planning on personally manufacturing him something more aesthetically pleasing later.

He hadn't asked Dennis's opinion, certain that the AI would rant for more than an hour about the lack of *feng shui*.

However, even if Rosey never got around to rebuilding this portion of *Aisha*, Moe was still happy (and grateful!) to be home.

Even with the differences.

Then again, *he* was different.

Donning the prince's robes (because Moe thought of the prince as a being separate from him) and playing the role to the hilt (channeling one of his older, snobbier uncles) had reminded Moe of the importance of family. Of connections.

Of money, but pretty much everything reminded him of that.

Including the fact that Constantine hadn't bothered to pay off the bank loan that Moe had with *Aisha*, and the next payment was due soon. The merchant's clock sitting on the control panel was a constant reminder.

He was going to have to start looking for work. Possibly in this system, but more likely, someplace nearby. Maybe hire some temporary help for Atilio, who had his hands full integrating the new systems and the old.

Possibly replace more of the of interior of *Aisha*, though he was not going to take up Dennis on his generous offer to help. The AI might not believe him when Moe told him yet *again* that he didn't want his personal cabin reflecting the prince.

However, Moe was willing to admit that the ship could use some freshening up. Some new paint. In the kitchen, new appliances. The sonic cleaners needed an upgrade. And...

Moe shook off his introspection. Before Atilio could come up here and accuse him of brooding. Or something like that.

A little light in the upper corner of the new console beeped. It took Moe a moment to realize that someone was hailing the ship. He slipped around and into the pilot's seat before he answered.

"Permission to come aboard?" came Jun's flirty tones.

"Of course!" Moe said, already standing up. "Uhm, where are you?"

"I'm in a flitter, flying from *The Roadrunner*, headed your way," Jun said.

"What if I'd forbidden you permission to board?" Moe teased.

"Oh, I'm certain we could come to a mutually beneficial agreement," Jun said. "My prince."

Moe sighed and rolled his eyes. Though he'd asked for all evidence of his crime to be destroyed, he knew that Dennis wouldn't. Particularly not after he'd declared the costume the pinnacle of his achievements to date.

Plus, there was that recording that Dennis had of the conversation he and Jamaal had had with Ellis on the station.

Hopefully, none of it would ever be used against Moe in a court of law.

He had no hope that Dennis hadn't gleefully shared every single bit of it with Jun.

"Fine, I'll meet you in at the airlock," Moe said resigned.

He did have a present for her, after all.

He picked up the silent necklace that held Sano's personality. The goons hadn't stripped the interior of the ship, despite Moe's fears. Maybe they'd taken one look at it and decided that there wasn't anything worth stealing.

The flitter landed precisely in the cargo bay. Had Jun been flying it? Or had Dennis been piloting it remotely? The latter, he was fairly certain. He wasn't about to ask, though. Questioning a woman's piloting skills was about as bad as asking her age.

Jun waited inside the flitter as the outer airlock closed and pressure in the cargo bay was re-established. Only after Moe opened the door to the interior of the ship did she open the door of the flitter.

Moe found himself breathing a sigh of relief when he saw Jun in what he thought of as "normal" clothes—shirt, vest, and baggy trousers, all done in beiges and browns—instead of her princess robes.

"My lady," Moe said as he crossed the floor of the bay over to her. He gave her a slight bow.

"My prince," Jun said in response, giving him a wicked grin.

Moe just rolled his eyes at her. He trusted that she wouldn't tease him about that too much.

"I have a gift for you," he said, handing her the necklace with Sano.

"Thank you!" Jun exclaimed. She clutched the necklace to her chest for a moment, whispering words that Moe couldn't hear.

A moment later, Sano's voice spoke loud and clear. "Hello Jun. I'm glad you could recover me."

"Me too," Jun said. "Do you have everything from the sliver?"

"I do," Sano said. "You've had quite the adventure, haven't you?"

"Don't tell," Jun said with a grin.

Though Sano had no physical appearance, Moe could practically hear the eyeroll.

"As if," the AI said dryly.

Jun slipped off the other necklace that she'd been wearing —the sliver that had contained only part of Sano's personality and data—and put it into a pocket.

Moe realized that Jun hadn't been pressing the full Sano to her chest, but to the other device.

"I have to ask—why put Sano into Atilio's room?" Moe said. He hadn't been hurt that she hadn't put it in his room.

No, really.

"Atilio was in the military," Jun said slowly. "Anyone looking at his space would see that. Everything was completely neat and tidy. Atilio would never hide anything in that room. So even if Constantine's goons had searched the ship, they would have left Atilio's room for last, then done a half-assed job of it, because it so very obviously wouldn't have contained anything."

"Smart," Moe said. He was pretty sure that his room had been searched. It hadn't been trashed—everything had been put back into place approximately where it had been found. A few things felt as though they were out of order, though. Like the tablet that had been on his nightstand was now on his desk.

"I have a proposal for you and Atilio," Jun said seriously.

"Let's go meet in the kitchen, then," Moe suggested. He called Atilio on the comm, asking him to come up, then walked with Jun to the small galley.

"Would you like some tea?" Moe asked while they waited.

The kitchen was still too large for just the pair of them, fit instead for a full crew.

Maybe someday he'd be able to afford them. At least for the time being, there would be fewer repairs necessary for *Aisha*. If he could find another cargo soon, they might actually be able to start digging themselves out.

"Tea would be lovely," Jun said. "How's *Aisha*?"

"She's good," Moe said as he poured the water. "The air filters are fixed, so it smells better now. And she flies well." That had been the first thing he'd noticed, just how responsive the ship was now.

Not that she'd ever been sluggish or bad. Just that she was better, now.

Atilio showed up and collapsed into a seat. Moe first handed Jun a cup of tea, then pushed one toward Atilio.

It was an Assam tea, heavily caffeinated, with lots of mint, ginger, and black pepper.

"Nice," Atilio said after the first sip, already straightening up. "So what's up?"

"I'd like to hire the pair of you to transport the alien artifacts to Ishiman," Jun said seriously. "All the alien artifacts."

Moe felt his eyebrows climb at that. "All of them?"

Jun gave a smug smile. "Yes. I need to keep working on the data chip. As I will be riding with you."

"Are you sure?" Moe said. "We're still doing shake-down runs. It will take us a lot longer to reach Ishiman than if you flew on *The Roadrunner.*"

"I am certain," Jun said. "I want to hire you. And to pay you for hauling the artifacts."

She quoted him a price that was about three times what Moe normally took for such cargo.

More than even Constantine would have paid.

Moe just gaped at her.

"That is the going rate for hauling royal cargo," Jun grinned. "Unless you think that isn't enough?" she added, going for innocent and missing by a mile.

"We'll take it," Atilio said before Moe could find his tongue again.

Jun smiled at him sunnily.

Moe knew he needed to take the deal. *Knew* that they needed the money. Knew that Jun probably was actually quoting him the going rate for royalty, and wasn't paying him extravagantly well.

His pride wasn't sure he could accept it, though.

"I know this is far above what you're normally paid," Jun said quietly. "Think of it as hazard pay."

"Hazard pay?" Moe said, finally finding his words again.

Jun nodded, suddenly serious.

"You're more of a target if you're carrying all the alien artifacts," she said. "Oswald could be coming after us. Or someone else."

"Then you shouldn't be riding with us," Moe said. "I don't want to put you into danger."

"Ah, but I'm your insurance policy if something does happen," Jun said. "No one will harm you if I'm here. Not without setting off an inter-governmental incident."

"So you're putting yourself into harm's way? Just to protect us?" Moe said, feeling his chest tighten.

The smile Jun gave him made his heart flutter as well as his anxiety kick in harder.

"I am," she said.

Moe nodded, feeling the weight of all that responsibility settle on his shoulders.

He'd keep her safe. Get her to Ishiman in one piece.

Or die trying.

TWENTY-TWO

Duri could barely keep herself from cackling with glee over the images she'd just received. However, the recording devices under her office desk would pick up that maniacal laughter, and that might cause someone to look too closely at what exactly Duri was up to.

Instead, she took a deep breath, calming herself, then another sip of tea before she gathered up the printouts again.

That ridiculous bribe she'd paid to that pirate was already reaping more rewards than she could have hoped for.

The alien control board was interesting enough just by itself. The image he'd sent her had high enough resolution that she could focus in on the alien writing sketched into pieces on the board.

It didn't look like any known Human script, that was for certain. Square, blocky letters. Maybe something like numbers. Who knew?

However, the other piece was worth all those credits.

A glowing data chip that was obviously of alien manufacture.

What secrets did it hold?

There were also a few pictures of a hastily-put-together machine. Maybe something that Rosey and the others had hacked together for reading the data chip? Was that why she'd gone to the Psykee system in the first place?

The images didn't arrive with any text. No explanation of what had happened, or what she was seeing.

They were followed by a series of numbers that Jun quickly determined were coordinates and dates.

As well as a ship's call numbers.

Damn it! The last one was only a day away.

Though Duri was good, and had enough credits in her department's pot to scramble a retrieval team, it would take too long for her team to get to the right location, clear at the far end of Allied Worlds' space.

No, she needed access to a team who could either move faster, or who possibly were already (illegally) in the area.

Damn it all to the various hells her grandparents still believed in.

She sighed, but she knew what she needed to do.

May as well see if General Carrick could be of any use and not just an impediment.

Duri put in a call to him directly, not bothering to have her office contact his office, for her people to set up something with his people. She needed answers now.

Surprisingly, the general answered the call himself. Personally.

Huh. Maybe he was taking her seriously.

"I have some important news regarding the project I'm researching," Duri told him promptly.

As there was only one thing that they were working on

jointly, he didn't need anything more than that over an open line.

"Is it urgent?" the general asked, sounding cordially gruff.

"Yes," Duri said. Really, she wouldn't have called if it hadn't been.

"I have a meeting in ninety minutes," the general responded. "If you can make it here before then, I'll talk with you."

"I'll be there as soon as I can get there," Duri promised before she signed off.

Really, it would be better if the general would have volunteered to come to her. She hated having to carry this sensitive information all the way across the government complex.

However, she didn't see any other choice. He *had* to see these pictures in order to appreciate the gravity of her request, how urgent her need was.

At some point, though, the general and everyone else would be dancing to *her* tune. Not the other way around.

Duri had a special waterproof case that she slid the papers into, as the weather on New Rome had once again flipped and it was positively soggy outside. She didn't bother with more than a raincoat for herself, an umbrella being awkward to carry and possibly slowing her down.

She regretted that decision as soon as she stepped out into the sheets of rain.

No going back now.

Duri hustled her way across the familiar walkways. At least there weren't many idiots like her trying to get from one building to the next. No, they all waited for the trundling cars that made their looping route, being covered, seated, and comfortably dry.

The general was just going to have to put up with her squelching into his office. Maybe dripping water onto his spotlessly clean floor. Soaking his utilitarian, uncomfortable guest chairs.

Those sorts of thoughts kept her warm, if not dry, on her trek.

The general's secretary appeared to be waiting for her, and issued her directly in to see the general.

Nothing had changed in the room—still sparse, still unremarkable, still plain enough that it bordered on a monk's cell.

The general, though, had a brightness to him, as if Duri's suppressed excitement had infected the man.

"What do you have for me?" he asked, his black eyes staring at her briefcase, perhaps seeing could drill holes in it to see what was inside.

"Images of artifacts that appear to be truly alien in nature," Duri said, unable to resist telling him the truth.

She plopped down in one of the guest chairs with her raincoat still on so the water would soak into the inadequate cushions. Then she unlocked her case and drew out the papers.

"These are from the contact I told you about, the one embedded in Rosey De Vries' group," Duri said as she slipped the printouts across the desk.

The general nodded as he studied the first photos of the alien board. His eyes widened at the blowup that Duri had done of the alien characters on what looked like transmitters.

He didn't look up until he saw the data chip. The still image had managed to capture the fact that the chip somehow glowed, casting shadows against the hand holding it.

"Where are these items currently?" he asked.

"Still in De Vries's possession," Duri said. "However, I have also received a set of dates and coordinates, where the artifacts will be. They are on route to Ishiman at this time, in a freighter."

"I see," the general said, examining the last paper Duri gave him.

He sighed, nodding. "We can make this last one."

Duri gave him a tight smile. "Good," she said.

"Are they armed?"

Duri wanted to lie about how dangerous this target was, how his men needed to be prepared to lay down their lives to acquire these precious artifacts.

However, she knew that they were unarmed. The ship's call numbers were registered to a tramp freighter owned mostly by a bank in the Allied Worlds, nominally licensed to a Mohammed Abdul Nuwan Pradeep Aruna Tennakoon Herath. The ship had no fighting capabilities whatsoever.

"No, they aren't armed," Duri said after a few moments. "At least not as far as the latest records of the ship show." It was a broken-down old freighter. It would make more sense to sell the piece of junk and start afresh rather than trying to rebuild it from scratch, including arming it.

"My men will still be prepared," the general said. "Thank you for bringing this to my attention."

Duri stiffened at the apparent dismissal. "May I ask a favor?"

The general gave a genial nod of his head, the implication being that while he might listen to a request, there was no guarantee that he'd actually fulfil it.

"Can you collect my asset at the same time?" Duri asked innocently enough. "I'd like to thank him personally for bringing us the alien artifacts."

The general looked a bit perturbed at that.

Yes, that was exactly what Duri had thought. Possibly he'd

planned on bringing in the boy already and just not telling Duri about it. Maybe even converting him to be the general's lackey, instead of Duri's.

"Fine," the general said after a few moments.

Good. Now, it was a waiting game. Again.

As long as the general's men didn't screw up too badly.

TWENTY-THREE

Dennis was *not* pouting about no longer officially (or even unofficially) being a royal escort.

Really.

Sure, fine, maybe he understood about Jun wanting to travel over on *Aisha* with Moe. Even he could see that she was smitten with the prince.

So *maybe* Rosey had had to point that out to Dennis. And he'd had to go back through his records, paying careful attention to where Jun focused her attention. And how her heart rate had elevated slightly at the sight of Moe, or even the mere mention of his name.

Shame that he wasn't an actual prince.

Not that Jamaal was putting some kind of plan in place to make it a reality. Dennis wouldn't know anything about that.

In the meanwhile, why in the world was Rosey making a mess in his cargo area? More of a mess than usual?

It wasn't surprising that she was taking apart a flitter. She did that regularly enough. Weighing the pieces hadn't made much sense to him, but he'd obliged and helped her get the perfect weights out of jumbles of parts.

Then everything, including all the green and white shipping containers, got put into a cargo flitter provided by Moe. Evidently, it was the same one that had originally collected the containers on that alien world, where they'd picked up Jun.

Still, Rosey had left such a mess behind. Not only that, she'd insisted that Dennis not disturb any of the papers or boxes still stacked in the hold.

Fine. Even though they were in hyperspace, flying between worlds, Dennis could still do something about it.

At least Jamaal had been willing to act as Dennis's "hands" and to put up the wall partitions Dennis had in storage. Generally, they were used to hide construction areas so that Rosey wouldn't complain too much about whatever work Dennis had hired contractors for.

"So, Jamaal," Dennis said, watching as the man worked. "Why exactly did Rosey agree for Ajax to fly the princess's ship back to Ishiman?"

It had all seemed so abrupt, how everyone had split apart, with Ajax going off on his own, Moe, Atilio, and Jun to *Aisha*, just leaving Jamaal and Rosey here on *The Roadrunner*.

Jamaal grinned. "What, do you miss him?"

Dennis snorted. "No. Not in the least. However, I do have the capacity to fly that ship myself, you know. It wouldn't have taken much effort to yoke us together."

Jamaal nodded. "I was a little surprised that the princess didn't have a more intelligent ship that could fly itself. I had never considered that she'd have to pilot it herself."

"Princess Jun doesn't actually bother with such details," Dennis informed Jamaal with maybe a touch of haughtiness. "Her governess, Sano, actually does the flying for her."

"Ah, that makes more sense," Jamaal said.

Now that Dennis had met the entire AI, and not just the small sliver, he'd been much more impressed by her capabilities.

Of course, she wasn't as magnificent as *he* was. Still, she had a job to do and she was capable of performing it well. Which, coming from Dennis, was actually high praise.

"So why didn't Rosey have me fly that ship?" Dennis persisted in asking. *It* was an officially registered royal transport. The least Dennis could do was to drag the idiot along.

"Well, Ajax did perform well while he was here," Jamaal said.

"I know," Dennis grumbled. "Didn't once get 'lost' or try to access a part of the ship that he shouldn't have." Not that Dennis had been waiting for him to screw up. No, the "littlest pirate," as Atilio called him, had been polite, always doing what Dennis or anyone else asked of him, never being too much of a nag.

Except when it came to flying the princess's ship.

"And he didn't send any messages while he was here on *The Roadrunner*, right?" Jamaal said.

"True," Dennis said with a sigh. There had been some messages sent out after Ajax had gotten onto the princess's ship, but he hadn't detected anything suspicious in those.

"I still don't trust him," Dennis continued.

Not even in a locked and boobytrapped airlock, cut off from everything and everyone.

Possibly not even one without any air in it.

"We don't necessarily trust him either," Jamaal said. "Sometimes, though, you have to give people enough rope to hang themselves with."

He straightened out the screen he'd just set up.

Before Dennis could mention it, Jamaal pushed in the far corner, so the screens were perfectly lined up.

"Thank you," Dennis said. He already felt better with that clutter pushed over there. Now, he wouldn't be ashamed the next time the princess boarded the ship.

"I know that Atilio is still testing the engines on *Aisha*," Dennis said as Jamaal started doing some sort of martial arts moves in the hold. The dojo might have been better, but perhaps Rosey was using it. "But do we really have to drop out of hyperspace every four hours or so?"

"The princess is over on *Aisha*," Jamaal said. "Don't want to risk her getting shredded, now, do we?"

"Which is why she should be over here where it's safe!" Dennis complained.

"We're following behind them," Jamaal reminded him. "If something happens to that ship, we'll be along to pick up the survivors."

Dennis couldn't help but sighing. It still made no sense to him.

Ajax and his ship were flying close to *Aisha*, closer than *The Roadrunner* was. When they came out of hyperspace, Dennis and the rest would be almost a full day away from the princess! Stretchsuits would probably keep everyone alive and well if there was an accident, but it still grated on him that they weren't closer. Doing small hyperspace jumps within a system wasn't really possible given the physics.

And Rosey was a good enough pilot that he knew it wasn't a mistake.

Well, at least they were almost finished with the slow jumps. In a day or so, they'd finally be back in Empire territory and start making longer ones.

They came out of hyperspace with a *plop*. Or at least that

was what Dennis always "heard" when they arrived. Not that hyperspace meant that much to him. There was less to do there, so he generally spent the time perfecting his designs.

Most recently, he'd been dabbling in architecture, creating incredible palaces for the princess and her prince.

Dennis sent out his sensors as soon as they arrived in system.

There was *Aisha*. And yes, still close to a day's travel ahead of them.

The princess's ship was close by.

Wait.

So was another ship.

One of those ugly Kollective Defenders.

Dennis sounded the alarm.

Hopefully, they could speed across the distance between the ships and arrive before it was too late.

TWENTY-FOUR

Atilio grinned when this time, after *Aisha* breached regular space, his boards remained clear.

Those new engines that Constantine had thoughtfully supplied were working great. Finally.

He still wanted to go back and string up whoever had initially wired the engines. Sure, the job had been adequate. It had also been sloppy. Wires hadn't been soldered or tied down, but instead, left to dangle. The interface was a kludge at best and likely to error out instead of sending the ship anywhere.

Don't even get him started on that console that Moe was supposed to use to pilot the ship.

In addition, there had been the numerous reporting trackers that Atilio had had to kill. Fortunately, those, too, had been clumsily added and easy to trace.

As far as he (and Rosey, and Dennis) could tell, Constantine's goons hadn't gotten around to injecting any ITTs into the metal of the ship itself. They'd been relying on the ship's software to tell them where *Aisha* had gone. No hardware, at least none that Atilio had found. (Yet. He wouldn't stop being paranoid about it, well, ever, but he would ratchet everything down a notch after nine—no, twelve—months or so.)

It was one of the reasons why they were taking their time on this trip. Atilio would clear the last of the trackers out, they'd go into hyperspace for a while, pop back out, and he'd have to go kill a few more.

Even though this time his screen was clear, and not showing any new trackers, he didn't assume that everything was clean yet. Constantine may have stuck some time-delayed trackers that Atilio was just going to have to out-stubborn.

He'd also kept himself to the engine room to give Moe and Jun a bit more time together. They were cute in a helplessly romantic sort of way.

Despite Moe playing at being a prince, he really wasn't at Jun's level. The only one truly on their side was Sano, who thought the two crazy star-crossed lovers might have a chance.

Atilio hoped that they would, but he'd be there for Moe if (when) his world came crashing down on him. As Moe had been there for him.

An alarm suddenly rang, echoing loudly in the engine section that Atilio had sequestered himself. He started so hard he banged his head against the back of the space. Swearing at himself, Atilio hoisted himself out of the engine space and went running for the helm.

Jun was already there, standing behind Moe.

A large ship loomed nearby.

A Kollective Defender. Big, blocky, intimidating.

There was no way in hell that they'd be able to outrun it. Their new engines hadn't been tuned well enough.

Give Atilio enough time, a big enough budget, and access

to a really good workshop (like Rosey's) and he'd be able to make those tweaks.

Not today.

"Friends have decided to join our party," came Ajax's cocky voice over the comm. "Now, before you do anything stupid, let us come over and explain everything to you."

Moe looked up at Jun, then Atilio. His eyes held a grim fatalism that put Atilio's back up.

"What are your orders?" Moe asked Jun quietly.

She nodded. "I was afraid this might happen," she said softly. "We let him come. I have...contingency plans."

"Good," Moe said darkly.

"And they do *not* involve you throwing your life away in some misguided attempt to save me or my work," she added sharply.

Atilio couldn't help but grin.

She had Moe's number, that was certain.

"Or you," she added, turning to glare at him.

Atilio held up his hands, giving up instantly. "Wouldn't dream of it."

Though the princess had explained why *Aisha* was carrying all the alien artifacts that the group had gone to so much trouble to collect, it just wasn't as safe here. Even her ship might have been better, though if Ajax and the others had attacked the princess's ship, it would have caused an intergovernmental incident. And yes, the Kollective might have been stupid enough to do that.

Them? They were cannon fodder. Literally and figuratively.

"Cargo bay unlocked and ready for visitors," Moe grumbled finally, letting Ajax know where to board.

"I'll kill him myself," Atilio volunteered as Moe turned to him.

"No," Jun said. "No killing." She glanced between the two men. "Not unless you have to," she added quietly.

Atilio looked at Moe and nodded.

As long as they were still breathing air, and not vacuum, they would be fine.

The three of them walked back to the cargo area.

Strange, Jun hadn't gotten into any of the containers since they'd arrived.

Then again, she did have the *new* alien artifacts to study. Which she did do, when she wasn't spending time with Moe.

Ajax came strutting onto the ship like the peacock that he was, as if he owned it. He was back to his pirate gear, a "tough boy" black leather vest that he wore without a shirt, sporting pale skin and what Atilio would bet were cyber-enhanced muscles. The boy wasn't about to push himself and actually do the work to maintain that physique.

Atilio kept his quiet growl to himself as half a dozen armed Kollective military grunts boarded behind the littlest pirate. They wore dark gray combat uniforms, heavily armored. They also carried lasers specially modified so they wouldn't shoot through the ship's shielding, but that would carve up people just fine.

"These are the boxes," Ajax said with an airy wave of his hand. Then he pointed at Jun. "She has the other pieces we need to collect."

"Not on her," Sano piped up.

The Kollective boys did hop to it impressively, suddenly pointing their lasers up, down, in every direction, uncertain where that voice had come from.

"Sano, you didn't have to say that," Jun said, sounding angry.

"Yes, I did," Sano said. "I knew it was foolishness to let you continue this way. I am the AI for Princess Jun Ogawa," she announced as the military men finally caught a clue.

"Princess Ogawa?" said one of the soldiers, stepping forward. Probably the lead for this group.

"That's right," Jun said, her chin going up defiantly.

Atilio didn't know if he was proud of her for not being cowed or wishing she'd keep her damned mouth shut.

"The pieces you're looking for are in her cabin," Sano instructed.

"Sano!" Jun said.

"It is my job to protect you," the AI replied. "Particularly when you don't appear to be doing a very good job of it yourself."

"I'll show you. Sir," Atilio volunteered as he stepped forward.

He'd give it to the soldiers. They all aimed at him as soon as he moved.

The man shot a hard glare at Atilio, then paused and nodded.

Good. He saw what Atilio was trying to portray through his tight stance: that he'd served and understood better than the civilians what the situation was.

"All right," the commander said, pointing to two of the men to follow Atilio. "Your friends will be sacrificed if there's any funny business."

"I understand, sir," Atilio said.

Ajax stepped up. "I'll go too, to make sure he gives us all the alien artifacts."

Atilio just glared at Ajax.

If looks could kill…

Atilio led the group down the corridor, sweating, aware of the target on his back.

Jun had been staying in the cabin Moe had originally put her in. Sentiment, perhaps? At least this time she could come and go as she pleased.

It was still mostly empty, with a bed, sanitizing closet, desk and chair.

Huh. It was a lot cleaner than the last time he'd poked his head in there. Almost all of the papers that had practically carpeted the floor were put away.

The alien artifacts were out on the desk, with just a slim folder holding papers. Along with the reader that Oswald had built.

"There you are, my beauties!" Ajax said, sweeping into the room.

Atilio nearly rolled his eyes. What if it had been booby-trapped? He hadn't stepped across the threshold.

However, Ajax didn't understand the implications of not going first.

The littlest pirate pulled out a couple bags made of shiny material.

Maybe he *had* learned something during his time with them. Those looked like the same sort of bag that Rosey had originally carried the pieces in, that blocked all signals.

Ajax carefully placed the alien circuit board in one, then the data chip and reader in a second.

And just because he was being a shit, he also swept up all the notes that were on Jun's desk.

Atilio kept his thoughts to himself as he led the soldiers back to the now empty cargo bay, the white and green containers already on their way to the Kollective ship.

"Did you retrieve everything?" the commander asked Ajax.

"Got all the booty right here," the boy said with a smarmy grin.

"We're done here," the commander said.

His men fell into line next to him.

Ajax stupidly paused in front of Jun. "That's a pretty bauble you have," he said. His hand was halfway raised to touch it when the commander was suddenly beside him.

"No," the man said, the word carrying the impact of an old lead-firing pistol. He grabbed Ajax's wrist. "You will *not* provoke an inter-governmental incident. Recovering stolen papers and precious alien artifacts can be explained away. Stealing directly from one of the royal house cannot."

Ajax glared at the man, then twisted his wrist.

The commander released Ajax's arm then stood there silently, staring impassively at the littlest pirate, as if he were daring the man to make one more stupid move.

"Fine," Ajax said. He stomped back toward the airlock like the petulant child he was.

"If I ever see you again, I'll kill you before you even get the chance to say a single word," Atilio told Ajax as the group prepared to leave.

Ajax held up a hand with the middle finger raised, not even bothering to turn around to look.

"Not if I see you first," he promised.

The soldiers left as professionally as they'd boarded.

Moe turned to Jun. "I'm so, so sorry," he said, his voice sounding broken.

Jun held up her hand, asking for Moe to hold his peace for a bit.

"Sano, are they gone yet?"

"Still traversing between the ships. Boarding the Defender.

Leaving the immediate area. And...they're gone," Sano said, bringing them play-by-play action. Her sensors were probably tied into *Aisha*'s, permission granted by Moe, Atilio would guess.

"Sano, give *The Roadrunner* the all clear message," she instructed as she turned to Moe and grinned up at him.

"I have a story to tell you."

TWENTY-FIVE

Itsuki went through the motions of the ceremony, celebrating the God of Fire's return after the long cold winter season. His hands picked up the chalice of oil, his fingers automatically dipping in to collect just three drops, before flicking them into the flame building on the altar.

While his body moved, his mind was elsewhere.

Fuming.

Stoking a fire big enough to take down the Empire itself.

Few attended the ceremony in the tiny chapel. Those who did probably had as little belief as Itsuki did and only celebrated the gods as their politics, not their spirits, moved them to.

No adornment marred the gray walls of the chapel. No windows, either. The roof, though sharply peaked, wasn't very tall. Even the pews were formed out of stone, though the congregation had insisted that cushions be allowed. The effect was cold and stern, only vaguely warmed by the fires that burned brightly in every corner.

Itsuki executed the ceremony with precision, sang the

prayers perfectly, and performed every movement flawlessly. The fire in the brazier leaped up for just a few moments as he spoke the benediction, before dying down to a small flame that Itsuki would ensure burned every day for the next year.

That was his official job in the court of the Emperor: to act as the head priest of the God of Fire. He blessed officials, attended births and birthday celebrations, and led the other priests in the prayers sung at the start of every season of the court, blessing the Emperor and all those who attended him.

Itsuki's real job was spymaster for the Emperor.

Few knew that.

His role as a priest enabled him to attend every court session, to listen and watch while at the same time, fading so far into the background that no one paid any attention to him.

It was the perfect cover, really.

Of course, the court sessions were recorded, and Itsuki spent time reviewing those records, verifying hunches and seeking clues. He also met with his spy chiefs, running their networks through the vast reaches of space, amongst all one hundred and nine planets that owed their allegiance to the Empire. And he trained his body to remain a formidable weapon, despite having just turned sixty that year. He dyed his hair black to hide the silver creeping into it, used creams on his face to hide the wrinkles, as well as lotions to remove the age spots in his hands. He wore formal gray robes that fully covered him from neck to wrist to ankle, with only the smallest of fire designs along the edges.

Itsuki did his job well. Worked in the shadows and never stepped into the light, despite tending the flames of the God of Fire.

However, it was possible he'd been standing back too far, as it appeared that the Emperor had forgotten his spymaster when he'd made the last round of promotions.

Not that Itsuki expected to be promoted.

But his son, Kaito, should have been. Not that frimpy prince, Minato.

Itsuki calmly stood at the door of the tiny chapel and said goodbye to his parishioners, wishing blessings on them. Most hurried out, not wanting to waste more time doing their pious duty. A few of the older women lingered, chatting and smiling with him. One even let him know that the ceremony had certainly warmed up her old bones, giving him a leer.

Itsuki let that comment slide without the appropriate eyeroll. Though priests were not required to be celibate, since his wife had divorced him, he hadn't bothered finding other companionship, but had instead done as she'd suggested and buried himself further in his work.

Work that wasn't being acknowledged as it should have been.

Itsuki strode back inside the chapel, not locking the door behind him, as much as that galled him occasionally. The chapel was to be accessible by all, at all times. A place where people could come and pray as they felt the need.

He did activate the defensive mechanisms. Everyone who walked through the door was immediately scanned, their biometrics used to identify them. If someone entered who wasn't supposed to be in there, who couldn't be found on the network, or if someone entered carrying weapons, a silent alarm would be set off, alerting the palace guards.

The flame on the altar still burned, fed by the small tube of gas connected to the brazier. In ancient times, the priest and his or her acolytes would have to maintain that light, feeding the flame by hand. Too many terrible stories were told about empires who employed lazy servants to tend to the gods.

Itsuki contemplated that flame.

It was his job to protect it. To protect the Empire.

What the latest leader appeared to have forgotten was that Itsuki worked for the good of the whole, not for the Emperor himself.

And that he should have been rewarded for such dedication.

His first attempt at rectifying the problem—by poisoning Prince Minato—hadn't gone as planned. One of his own spies had thwarted his plans.

There was a certain irony in that, which Itsuki did appreciate.

However, it wasn't to be allowed to happen again.

Itsuki had thought too small.

The entire Ogawa *family* would be shown to be untrustworthy. Unlucky. Not just the prince. But the daughter, Princess Jun, and the other son, the artist, Prince Daiki as well, would have to be disposed of.

Because while the Emperor was as modern as any man, he was also superstitious, something that Itsuki had encouraged. Emperor Ogawa believed strongly in luck.

A family who lost all their children, well, they're just *unlucky* and unlikely to receive any more favors from the court.

Itsuki could position his son Kaito as the perfect substitute. His son would shine in his new position. Grow more responsible as more responsibilities were given to him.

Of course, Itsuki could never tell Kaito that he was the one who'd arranged all of this. His son thought little of his father, accused him of being stodgy and old fashioned, of believing in gods who had no place in the modern age.

Itsuki wasn't going to extinguish the flame that still burned brightly before him on the altar.

However.

If the Emperor didn't see his faithful servant's worth after all this?

That flame wouldn't last long in the face of Itsuki's revenge.

TWENTY-SIX

Ajax sat in his room aboard the Kollective Destroyer, looking again at his "booty." The room wasn't too bad, though a little generic. Bed, sanitizing closet, and desk, all in shades of military green. He'd asked about an officer's bunk—he knew they had a sitting room and maybe even a galley kitchen—but he'd been told they were all in use.

At least that jackass of a commander had allowed him to keep what they'd acquired and hadn't insisted on locking it up.

Hadn't even been treating Ajax too badly either.

He grinned to himself.

It was good to have powerful friends. And he had no doubt that Duri Chang was about as powerful as it got.

That she'd managed to find him, locate the debt on *Hermes 3.0*, and give him enough credits to pay off the ship had been quite a feat by itself.

Then she'd stayed out of his way. Treated him like the professional that he was.

He already had the parts he needed for the job she'd

proposed. Those stupid geeky T-shirts had been useful so often.

No one looked too closely at the anime characters on those shirts.

Or the huge eyes they had, which worked well as cameras. Passive data collection that would slip by most sensors.

Plus, he'd been accepted at that point by Rosey and the others. He'd proven his worth to them by helping stage the break-in of Oswald's fortress. As well as stealing back Moe's ship.

Despite that, he'd been careful. Played his role as a young man, his father's son.

He'd minded his temper, his language, and his curiosity.

Instead of being the badass pirate he truly was.

Now, his bank debts were cleared. He'd not only raced Rosey De Vries, he'd traveled on her infamous ship for a while, *The Roadrunner*. Sure, he might have made some enemies.

What pirate didn't?

He wasn't thrilled about traveling all the way into the Kollective. Probably Duri had another job for him. Something that only a badass pirate like he could handle.

He looked again at the parts they'd acquired. There really wasn't much to see on the circuit board. It was just another board. Maybe someone, somewhere, could make sense of it. That was what you paid other people for.

The data chip still felt the same, as if it had been manufactured out of smooth glass. It didn't glow as much now as it once had. Maybe the internal power supply was running down.

Duri Chang would know what to do with it.

And she would reward him appropriately as well.

Ajax put away his items and lay back in his bunk.

The future was surely going to be bright.

TWENTY-SEVEN

Instead of flying full speed across the system they'd been in, Rosey agreed to make the next hyperspace jump, putting them all in a fairly deserted part of Empire-controlled space.

At least this time, she'd allowed Dennis to place them very close to *Aisha*, so it was easy for the others to fly over to *The Roadrunner* and have a chat.

Rosey had wanted to fly directly to Ishiman at this time, but Jun had insisted that everyone needed to get together and talk first.

Rosey had agreed, and not just because she wanted to see Atilio again. Sure, he was a good mechanic, and as much of a gear-head as she was. And she was getting used to being around a guy who was about her height, instead of taller than her.

He wouldn't be around for much longer, though, now that Moe had *Aisha* back. They'd be on their way, searching for their next cargo.

While she and Jamaal would continue on their hunt for the aliens.

The flitter arrived and their three visitors entered. Moe just glared at Rosey—probably still angry that she hadn't bothered to let him in on the secret. Atilio gave her an apologetic shrug, whereas Jun demanded, "Where are they?"

Rosey grinned. "They're with Jamaal. Come on."

They all trooped into the eating nook, where Jamaal sat with the actual alien artifacts on the table. Jun rushed over to them, holding them up and examining them carefully.

"Dennis, I must say you made really good facsimiles of these," Jun said, smiling.

"Of course, my lady," Dennis said. "It is always a pleasure to serve you."

Rosey didn't roll her eyes, but just barely.

"Why weren't we told about the switch?" Moe blurted out.

Rosey was sure that Jun had already told him, but he probably wanted to hear it from her.

"It was my decision," she said as they all crowded in around the table. The space really was better for four people.

She could already hear the pleas from Dennis about being able to expand the area.

"I know you may have the acting chops. But you might not. I wanted to make sure that you both acted accordingly, when you were boarded," Rosey said simply.

"You trusted Jun," Moe pointed out.

"Wouldn't have told her either, if I could have gotten away with it," Rosey said with a shrug. "And while Dennis's copies were good, they wouldn't have fooled her."

Atilio nodded, satisfied. Moe still frowned, but he'd come around. Or he wouldn't.

"She didn't even bother to let *me* in on the secret," Dennis complained to the group.

That shook Moe out of his brood. "Really?"

Rosey shrugged. "I'm good at computer security. My

systems are tight. Doesn't mean they couldn't be hacked. We always flew at a distance in part because of that. But also, so that the Kollective ships wouldn't hang around. Particularly when we started approaching. At speed."

While Dennis's assessment of it taking twenty-four hours for them to cross the space between the ships, that was only going at regular speeds.

At top speed, they could have done it in three, maybe four hours.

Rosey had kind of been looking forward to doing that, but it had made more sense for both ships to hop away and meet someplace else.

That got nods from both Moe and Atilo.

"We did trust you enough to believe that you'd stick with us, and not suddenly turn into Kollective agents," Jamaal added.

That got more nods.

"Can't ever say I won't do it again, but I'll try not to," Rosey said. Though she wasn't sure how much that mattered, as she didn't know when she'd see them again, after they dropped their cargo off at Ishiman.

"The Kollective soldiers were professionals," Atilio said. "Probably the only reason we didn't have any issues."

That surprised Rosey. Then again, the rot probably didn't set in until the upper levels.

"In the meanwhile, we won't ever have to worry about Ajax again," Rosey said. "He's going to be in a military prison for life once Duri realizes how she's been tricked."

Jun gave her a grin at that. "Thank you for filling those containers with enough material to make them still seem full. What did you use, by the way?"

It was Rosey's turn to grin. "Flitter parts. You'll find all your original artifacts from the dig, and your papers, still in the cargo bay."

"That's what's behind those walls I had Jamaal set up?" Dennis said.

"You could have looked at them more closely," Rosey drawled.

She could only imagine the *hmph* that Dennis gave as he reviewed whatever security tapes that might have shown the switch she'd made.

"But what was so important that we needed to meet now? While we're still in space, and not at Ishiman?" Rosey said, turning to Jun. "What was so important that you didn't want to risk talking about it on an open channel?"

Jun turned serious. Rosey saw the edges of the princess appear as she drew herself up, like she probably would before addressing the royal court.

"Before I stowed away and met all of you lovely people, I was working on Niala, the alien world where the Atoylee aliens once lived," Jun said. "Before it was destroyed."

"Wait, didn't the Atoylees destroy themselves in some sort of civil war?" Rosey had to ask.

Jun grimaced. "There's always been a debate about that. Maybe the Atoylee had that level of technology. Or maybe they didn't. I've always thought they'd been attacked, given the consistent ash layer and bomb craters that envelop the entire planet."

Rosey nodded. That made sense, though it was possible that the aliens had been about as smart (and as hotheaded) as Humans had been before they'd discovered a way off planet.

"So, in the Atoylee papers, there's mention of the Bukoykan," Jun explained. "The Atoylee had two different alphabets that they used: an older glyph set and a phonetic set that was used to phonetically spell out foreign words. Bukoykan was obviously a foreign word as it doesn't really follow the etymology of any of the Atoylee words that we know of."

Rosey nodded, following along.

"Now, I've been going through all the transcripts that we've so far managed to get out of the data chip," Jun said. "There is more data on that chip, more than just the spoken records. Possibly starting coordinates, as we'd originally guessed. Their system of measurement is going to be different than ours, though, so once we retrieve that data, it's still going to take some time to figure out an exact location."

Rosey wasn't going to ask Jun to get to her point. She could be patient. No, really.

"Anyway, there's more than one flight recorded on the chip. The last one, well, it's kind of hair raising."

She plugged the data chip into the little reader, toggled a few micro-switches, and suddenly, the words of an alien voice filled the small nook.

"I can only take it from the start of the recording," Jun said apologetically. "However, as far as we can ascertain, the same words are repeated at the start of every recording. Some sort of flight checklist."

Rosey had given Jun her own list, along with a couple of other standard ones, so they could possibly start to guess as to which controls the pilot was talking about.

The words were understandable at first. Everything normal. A list of items being asked and answered.

After a short while, Rosey felt as though the words grew tense. Every syllable was chopped off. There was a lot more growling.

Followed by yelling. And more yelling.

Things were really going wrong for the pilot of this craft.

"There," Jun said. She stopped the recording. "Listen carefully."

Rosey turned her head so that her right ear was closer to the table.

The recording started again.

Wait. That word that the pilot was shouting. It sounded familiar.

At least there wasn't a horrific dying scream at the end. The recording just cut out.

Rosey peered at Jun, who nodded.

"Yes. I don't know for certain. However, I believe that at the end, he's saying that someone is attacking him. Possibly an alien race called the Bukoykan. The same one that attacked the Atoylee."

Sign up for my newsletter and I'll start you on your travels with a free copy of my book, *The Island Sampler.*

http://www.LeahCutter.com/newsletter/

ABOUT THE AUTHOR

Leah R Cutter writes page-turning fiction in exotic locations, such as a magical New Orleans, the ancient Orient, Hungary, the Oregon coast, rural Kentucky, Seattle, Minneapolis, and many others.

She writes literary, fantasy, mystery, science fiction, and horror fiction. Her short fiction has been published in magazines like *Alfred Hitchcock's Mystery Magazine* and *Talebones*, anthologies like Fiction River, and on the web. Her long fiction has been published both by New York publishers as well as small presses.

Find Leah's books on Knotted Road Press at (www.KnottedRoadPress.com)

Follow her blog at www.LeahCutter.com.

Reviews

It's true. Reviews help me sell more books. If you've enjoyed this story, please consider leaving a review of it on your favorite site.

Come someplace new...

Do you enjoy exploring strange new worlds, new cultures, new people?

Journey into the various lands envisioned by Leah R Cutter.

Sign up for my newsletter and I'll start you on your travels with
a free copy of my book, *The Island Sampler.*

I will never spam you or use your email for nefarious purposes.
You can also unsubscribe at any time.

http://www.LeahCutter.com/newsletter/

ABOUT KNOTTED ROAD PRESS

Knotted Road Press publishes dynamic fiction set in exotic locations. Our authors cover a wide range of genres including science fiction, fantasy, mystery, literary, and poetry. We also have unique non-fiction voices in genres such as autobiography, business, cookbooks, and how-tos. We offer both DRM-free ebooks and print books for a global readership.

Knotted Road Press
www.KnottedRoadPress.com

www.ingramcontent.com/pod-product-compliance
Lightning Source LLC
Chambersburg PA
CBHW070542100726
47907CB00004B/1231